EARL OF BRECKEN

ONCE UPON A WIDOW #5, WICKED EARLS' RETURN

AUBREY WYNNE

PLATO PUBLISHING

ISBN: 978-1-946560-21-6

Editing by The Editing Hall

Cover Art by Jaycee DeLorenzo

Formatting by Anessa Books

❀ Created with Vellum

PRAISE FOR ONCE UPON A WIDOW

Praise for Once Upon a Widow series

"Historically accurate with poignant characters dealing with strife so gut-wrenching, I can't even imagine how I'd respond. Gripping story with an explosive ending."
    N.N. Light Book Heaven Reviews

"Aubrey Wynne's epic historical romance bedazzles as much as it leaves the reader breathless! Her intricate details lavish the reader with picturesque landscapes, scrumptious dialogue, leaving nothing too small to define."
    InD'tale Magazine

"Somewhere between Austin and Heyer. A good read."
    Amazon review

"The scenes are so graphically detailed and descriptive, it paints an elegant backdrop that makes the storyline pop."
    Amazon Top 500 Reviewer

"This well-written piece has a balance of sorrow and happiness it will make you cry, smile, and maybe even jump with joy. I highly recommend this charmer."
    Vine Voice Review

"Aubrey wields her words as skillfully and precise as a surgeon with his scalpel."
    Amazon Top 1000 Reviewer

"I highly recommend."
    Jersey Girl Book Lover

"Another author for my favorite list."
    Amazon Top Contributor, Book Reviews

EARL OF BRECKEN

A seductive Welsh earl on the brink of ruin. A wealthy cit in search of a hero.

Miss Evelina Franklin reads too many romance novels. She's certain a handsome duke—or dashing highwayman—is in her future. In the meantime, Evie entertains herself with the admirers vying for her fortune.

The Earl of Brecken needs cash. His late father left their Welsh estate in ruin, and his mother will not let him rest until it is restored to its former glory. Notorious for his seductive charm, he searches the ballrooms for a wealthy heiress. His choices are dismal until he meets Miss Franklin. Guileless and gorgeous with an enormous dowry, she seems the answer to his prayers. Until his conscience makes an unexpected appearance.

Brecken Castle, Wales
November 1809

Madoc ran a hand over the horse's hindquarters, then moved his palm along the inside of the back-left haunch and found the swelling. He lifted the stallion's left hind leg. "Hold his head," he told the stableboy, "and when I release the leg, take him into a trot."

"Yes, my lord."

He counted to fifty, then let the hoof drop to the ground. The gleaming bay went into a trot with a noticeable limp, its hoof lightly scraping the dirt. "Now halt, back him up a dozen steps, then take him into a trot again."

The boy called over his shoulder. "Ye think it's only a spasm?"

"No, I think his stifle is locking up."

The horse moved forward without an issue. At fifteen, Madoc was known for his love of animals. He slept in a stall if a mare was foaling, spent an afternoon devising a splint for a sheep or goat with an injured leg, or wiled away hours with the chemist discussing human remedies that could apply to other species.

"Did you work your magic?" asked Lord Brecken, his hazel eyes twinkling gold in the afternoon sun. "Is he ready for the hunt?"

"I'm afraid not, Father."

"He looks fit to me." Brecken watched the huge gelding walk back toward the stable. "That's my favorite mount. If he's not lame, I'm riding him."

"I wouldn't, sir. I think that back joint may lock up after a strenuous ride, like it did today." Madoc took a deep breath and looked up at the towering earl. He hoped to match his father's height in the next few years. "Take my horse tomorrow. If I'm right, a bit of rest should take care of it."

"Ha! I'll ride my own, and if there's any trouble, I'll give him the rest of the month off." The earl smoothed back his dark hair and adjusted his hat. When he squinted up at the sun, the laugh lines deepened on his weathered face. He gripped Madoc's shoulder and gave him an affectionate shake. "You're the only man in this county that would dare argue with me. Besides my dashing looks, you've inherited my audacity."

Madoc had never compared himself to this remarkable man. True, their features and coloring were similar, but their temperaments were wholly different. His father was gregarious, charming, and spontaneous, though Mama called it impatient. He was also a natural leader. And fearless. "Father, I—"

"And not a word to your mother. She'll be nagging me all night." Brecken strode away, his long legs quickly eating up the distance to the stable. The great coat strained against his broad back, and Madoc straightened his own shoulders as he watched the earl walk away.

"You've been doing that since you were old enough to walk behind him. Always in his footsteps, imitating every move and expression."

"Mama, how do you manage to sneak up on me like that? You're quiet as a fox hunting chicken."

She laughed, a tinkling sound that always reminded him of the porcelain bells his grandmother had loved. "Doc, what secret is he keeping this time?"

Madoc grinned at the nickname, given to him as a child, because he was always doctoring some creature. If he wasn't heir to an earldom, he'd have studied medicine. Instead, he would follow his father's path and go to Oxford, take the Grand Tour if the war was over, and eventually assume his place at Brecken Castle.

"It will do you no good to ignore me. I won't tell, I just need to prepare myself." Her dark gaze settled on him. "When I'm kept in the dark, it usually includes some level of danger."

"I'm more concerned for the horse."

The next day, he wanted to take back those words. His father got his way and rode his favorite horse. At first, Madoc thought perhaps he'd been wrong. The stallion held up well after a hard day's ride. Lord Brecken, irritated they'd lost the fox, raced one of the younger men back to the castle. Coming to a hedge, both men leaned over their mounts as the horses jumped.

Madoc's heart lodged in his throat as the earl's horse baulked, its back leg jutting out. Lord Brecken was pitched over the hedge. Struggling to breathe, Madoc kicked his gelding's flanks to catch up, waiting to hear his father's angry bellow. But it never came. On the other side of the shrubbery lay the twisted body of his hero. A scream, muffled and seemingly far away, sounded behind him.

Mama!

He turned his mount on its haunches and held up a hand to the approaching riders as he slid from the saddle. His voice sounded calm and commanding, and he wondered how that could be when he trembled like a frightened child on the inside. "Keep my mother on the other side until we know his condition."

An old friend of the earl nodded and intercepted Lady Brecken while Madoc and two other men crouched around the earl. He rested on his back, his head and one leg at an odd angle, eyes closed. Putting his ear close to his father's face and placing two fingers on his neck, he blew out a loud sigh of relief. "He's alive. Let's get him to the castle. Send someone for the physician."

Madoc closed his eyes as his mother's wails filled the silence. "Sweet Mary, is he...?" She almost fell from her horse and collapsed over her husband. "Wake up, love." Her voice rose as she shook him. "Wake up, damn you. Wake up!"

"Mama, he's alive. We need to get him home." He wrapped his arms around her and pulled her up. "I'd say his leg is broken, from the angle of it. We'll know more once he's been examined and wakes up."

Someone whistled, and the wagon following with refreshment rumbled along the uneven field. It took four men to gently lift Brecken onto the bed. Lady Brecken, skirts in one hand, scrambled up next to her husband. She wiped at her cheeks, then rocked back and forth, holding one of his giant hands in both of hers. He could hear her whispering to the earl as if he could hear her.

Madoc helped the physician set the broken leg. As the bones cracked and popped into place, he wondered how the pain did not stir his father. A glance at the physician reinforced his concern.

"Let's take it as a blessing that he didn't wake," said the doctor. "I'll stop in daily to check on his progress. He'll be able to tell us more once he's conscious again."

But it would be several days before the earl was coherent. When he did rouse, the entire household heard him. Cursing like Madoc had never heard before floated down the hall. He ran down the hall that morning, praising the Lord above for small miracles. While the words weren't for delicate ears, the sound of his father's voice had eased the tightness in Madoc's chest. Until he reached the bedroom.

Inside, his mother stood next to the four-poster bed, fists pressed to her mouth, shaking her head. The early rays of dawn shone on her wet cheeks. When her gaze locked with Madoc's, his stomach lurched.

"What is it?" he rasped, tying the belt of his banyan around his waist.

"I can't bloody move! I can't feel my bloody legs. By God, get that physician here NOW!" The earl waved a shaking hand at the door. "NOW!"

By that afternoon, it was determined the earl had lost the use of both legs. It happened sometimes with back injuries. Madoc remembered a pup that had to be put down when a horse stepped on it. His mind whirled, going over every accident, every ailment he could remember. There had to be something they could do.

The weeks passed, and Lord Brecken went from ranting to depression. "Shoot me. Give me the same mercy we give a loyal horse. I can't live as an invalid."

Never had Madoc heard the pleading in his father's voice. The thought of a gun to the earl's head made his stomach quiver. Would he find a way to do it? Not his father. Not the Earl of Brecken. Suicide was a coward's way out.

. . .

In the end, he wasn't sure what was worse. His father chose silence over death, rarely uttering a word. He continued to breathe but stopped living. Mr. Caerton, the steward, maintained the estate and lands. When he approached his mother about working with Caerton and taking over some of the earl's responsibilities, she refused to listen.

"Your father planned on instructing you. We'll have to wait until he's himself again. I can't imagine his reaction if you took over without his consent."

At eighteen, Madoc left for Oxford as planned. The earl managed farewell that came out a snarl. "Enjoy your youth while you can. Happiness is capricious and snatched from you in the blink of an eye."

"Doc, he doesn't mean it. He loves you," his mother soothed. "This is just so hard for a man like him."

"A selfish man, you mean. It's self-pity that keeps him strapped to that chair. He might as well be dead." He closed his eyes at her gasp, stunned at his vehemence. "I'm sorry, Mama. I didn't mean that. It's just—"

"I understand. Be patient, my dear." She laid a hand on his cheek. "He'll come back to us. I know he will."

"You've been saying that for three years." Madoc wrapped his mother in a fierce hug. "I pray you are right. For your sake."

"For all of our sakes," she murmured into his chest.

CHAPTER ONE

January 1819
London, England

*M*adoc shivered, pulled up the fur collar of his great coat, and adjusted his beaver hat. With a well-placed kick, he urged his horse into a canter. He wanted London far behind him. His manservant followed with the luggage, but he needed air and time to prepare himself mentally for the upcoming encounter. His last visit had been more like a stay in a mausoleum than one's boyhood home. His father's mumbled responses and lackluster eyes had not prompted any lively conversation—until the end.

"I've completed my final year of university. Are you sure you want me to leave again so soon?" Madoc leaned against the mantel, the smoldering peat in the grate hot against his riding breeches. The May sun poured through the floor-to-ceiling windows and mocked

the thin, dour man wrapped in heavy wool blankets. Where had the Earl of Brecken gone? That man had been larger than life with a booming laugh, an iron fist, and cunning wit. A man his son had looked up to, imitated, his every action geared toward the hope of gaining the glow of his father's approval. The kind of man who commanded attention merely by walking into a room. And therein lay the problem.

The silence stretched. Perhaps the earl had fallen asleep. His gaze fell on his father's bony fingers, clutching a shawl about his rounded shoulders, as if it were his last defense. Madoc swallowed as his father's hazel eyes narrowed. The brown and green flecks, passed down to his only son, sparked with anger.

"Every young man needs to see the world. It's part of your basic education. Do you think I'm unable to manage my own affairs because I cannot walk?" rasped the earl, pushing back a limp strand of gray from his forehead. "Do you think the inability to use these feckless limbs affects my brain?"

"No, Father, but I believe it has affected your spirit." He went down on one knee and took a cold, papery hand between his warm palms. "Please, let me take you for a ride in the carriage, get out and see some of your tenants. Your soul is in this land. It would do you good."

"I don't need you to take me anywhere. If I wanted to leave my home, I'd do it," bellowed the old man with surprising volume. His shoulders slumped as if the admonishment had depleted what little energy he'd possessed. "Go! Enjoy your youth while you have it. Lady Fortune is a capricious, evil female. You never know how long happiness will perch on your shoulder."

Madoc's jaw tightened as he gave the earl a rigid nod and left the room. Why was he surprised? Delaying his response to the Home office, he had hoped for one last bid to bring his father back to the land of the living. By God, he'd tried. He'd take the assignment with no remorse, and he'd work under one of England's most brilliant spymasters. At twenty-two, he was making a name for himself. The danger and intrigue made him feel alive, a welcome and vivid contrast to the quiet hills of the Welsh countryside.

His parents suspected nothing, assuming their son had come from his last year at Oxford rather than Belgium and the war. This "Grand Tour" would provide the perfect ruse to be abroad, his title gaining him entry into the right circles to mingle, charm, and... listen. Napoleon had been declared an outlaw and was wreaking havoc again. The Crown needed every available set of eyes and ears. It may be years before he was able to return. If he returned. Lord Risk was as fickle as Lady Fortune.

He stopped at the front door, his palm on the cold handle of the door as he looked over his shoulder, a final glance around his child-hood home. An ancient castle with the countess's modern touch. The large receiving hall had been paneled with oak, the stone floor covered with narrow, polished planks, and the windows enlarged to allow more light. The furnishings had come from London by way of France and Italy, the earl sparing no expense for his new, young wife. Painted silks and satins hung on the walls and dressed the glass panes.

"Must you leave, Doc? Can you not put off your trip for a year or so?" His mother appeared at his elbow, using his nickname to soften him, no doubt. He recognized the familiar martyred expres-sion creasing her face. Her slender fingers clutched his riding coat. "He was so looking forward to your visit."

Madoc snorted. "Mama, you know my passage has been paid. Father has been quite adamant that I go."

"You don't understand what he's been through, what it's like for him. He's bitter, that's all. If you stayed, he'd come round. I'm certain." Her onyx eyes watered, and she laid a hand on his cheek. Rays of light shed a halo about her black chignon, at odds with the growing venom in her tone. "Have you become one of those dandies, then? Looking for pleasure and living off your father's money and good name? He needs you now."

He ground his teeth, his jaw tense. "He's been like this for six *years. My presence for a few weeks will not produce a miracle. I will obey my father's wishes, ma'am."*

Madoc turned on his heel and stormed out the door. A chestnut gelding stood patiently waiting in the courtyard. He mounted and turned the horse to face the veranda, hooves and cobblestones reverberating in the warm afternoon air. "Good day, Mama." With a bow and sweep of his hat, he added, "Until we meet again."

Four years ago. Four long years.

So much had happened in that time. He'd changed, lost his naivete, his youthful optimism. His skills belonged more to a soldier than a titled landowner. He had a relentless grip on a sword, excellent marksmanship, and a wicked right punch. He could go days without sleep. His superiors regarded him as the man with a seductive smile and honey-like charm that could distract top officials—or their wives—while correspondence was pilfered in their own libraries for secrets that could hasten the end of the war. He'd become the perfect chameleon, as comfortable playing a discontented foot soldier or a common thief in the rookeries as he was the polished dandy spending his father's fortune.

It had taken its toll.

Madoc trusted few people, rarely heard a conversation or request without discerning a hidden implication or ulterior motive, and was bone-tired. He wanted to sleep until the sun was high in the sky. Ride across his childhood estate, nod at tenants, and have no greater worry than balancing the ledgers and deciding which country dance or dinner to attend. It was time to begin his life, the life he'd been born to, the life that had called to him when he'd stepped onto English soil again. Yes, he was ready for the role he had only pretended at the last four years.

※

Brecken Castle and estates

A tired and dusty Madoc trotted toward the village of Brecknock. He crossed the stone bridge, drawing in a renewed breath as the clear water rushed and splashed under the arches. The slate mountains and snow-capped peaks seemed to be stacked on top of each other, like a crowd trying to see over the next shoulder. They provided the perfect background for his brooding mood. Curiosity would greet him in the village. Enthusiastic waves and questions about the master when the tenants realized it was Lord Madoc riding through.

A frigid wind whipped at his face, and he hunkered inside his coat and cursed. Devil confound it, it was cold. A man awake on all suits would have waited for his coach and valet. The sun peeked out from behind a billowy, gray cloud. He squinted at the unexpected brightness, his vision watery, barely able to discern the outline of the small town looming in the distance. As he drew closer, Madoc blinked and wiped his eyes with his palms.

He slowed his chestnut gelding to a trot and made his way to the square, taking in the dilapidated buildings. The main thoroughfare—that made him chuckle as he thought of the hectic, paved streets of London—was dotted with people buying last-minute wares from closing vendors and hurrying home before dark. A growl in his belly reminded him he hadn't eaten since breakfast, but his attention focused on the derelict condition of Brecknock.

There were no inquiries or smiles. No hoorays or nods from the men. Filth trickled like a brown and yellow brook from an alley and puddled near the street. Roofs were in disrepair, and walls had been patched and patched again. The tenants' clothes were worn and shabby. What in blue blazes was going on? His lovely village had gone to ruin.

"Good day," he called out to the blacksmith he'd known since a boy. "I've just returned home and can't help but notice..." He made a long sweep with his hand to encompass the sight before him. "What happened?"

"Ask his lordship," boomed the man before ducking his head and removing his cap, "or the devil in his pocket."

"And does this devil have a name?"

"Aye, it's Caerton's eldest, Niall."

"He's taken over for his father, then?"

"He's taken... That's a true statement, to be sure." The man turned away and disappeared into his smithy.

"By God, I'll get to the bottom of this," Madoc yelled to the retreating figure.

Four generations of Caertons had managed the estate for the Earls of Brecken. The last time he'd seen Mr. Caerton, the old man had been in decline. Finding it difficult to maintain the physical responsibility of managing Brecken's vast holdings, he had begun training his oldest son, Niall, to replace him. Madoc had never liked youth growing up. He remembered the boy picking a fight, then cheating by throwing dirt in the other lad's eyes to win. Of course, that had been years ago. People change. He was living proof of that.

It got worse as he cantered toward the castle. The fields were overworked. At a glance, he knew there had been no rotation of land. Less fertile soil, fewer crops, less profit. Perhaps Caerton had died before he'd been able to instruct Niall in all aspects of management. He'd give the steward the benefit of the doubt until he had more facts. If the past years had taught him anything, it was that appearances could be deceiving. A mirthless laugh scratched his throat, thinking of the disguises he'd donned over the years.

Madoc kicked his horse into a gallop as he passed a paddock of thin plow horses. He was glad he'd come home. It was time to take over for his father and have a word with Niall Caerton. As he clattered onto the stone courtyard, the butler appeared at the door.

"Lord Madoc, it is so good to have you back." He held the door open as Lady Brecken rushed down the steps to greet him.

"Oh, my sweet son. The lord has answered our prayers. You've come home just in time."

CHAPTER TWO

Late February 1819
London, England

*E*velina wiggled her toes over the bathing tub, then plunged under the steaming water to drown out Mama's barrage of complaints. She grinned against the water, her mother's words now muffled, though the irritated tone broke the liquid barrier. Who would run out of air first? Evelina's heart pounded louder; her chest tightened. Then a thick strand of her hair went taut. *Yank!* She burst through the water, panting, and glared up at her mother.

"Evie, this is a serious conversation. Do not ignore me." Lady Franklin wagged an accusatory finger. "We need to find a husband for your sister. It will be a miracle, if you ask me, after the debacle of last season."

She sighed and pushed the wet curls from her face. "You know very well that was not her fault. That dastardly

14

viscount is a sniveling weasel of a man. *If* you could call him a man. He humiliated poor Fenella with that wager."

Lady Franklin sank back onto the bed as the maid held up a thick towel for Evelina. "I admit it was a mistake, sending her alone for her first season. We should have waited a year and had you both presented together, though that might have been frowned upon too. Who'd have thought she'd be so naïve?"

Evelina snorted. "She's as tall as most men and meticulous with ledgers. She's been raised like Papa's son, could run the business herself, and is open and honest in a conversation. Yes, Mama, what could possibly go wrong, throwing her to the wolves at Almack's?"

"Watch your tone, my girl." Lady Franklin wrung her hands. "It *was* painful to watch. She's so awkward."

"Any creature is awkward when out of their habitat." Evelina pulled the thick dressing gown around her and sat before the small hearth. Louella, her lady's maid, began combing out her long tresses. "Fenella is adamant not to marry at this point. She needs time to see that not all of London's bachelors are the devil's spawn."

"Evelina, such language!"

"Well, it's true." Her poor sister had been the object of a wager between a set of self-indulged Corinthians. The young viscount—dashing but short of stature—had accepted a dare that he could get any green girl alone and kiss her. The chums had hedged their bet and decided on Fenella, the most awkward and tallest of the season's new arrivals. It had taken him two weeks, and his cronies had hidden in the bushes to witness the cruel hoax. Evelina's fists clenched every time she thought of her poor sister abused by those egotistical oafs.

"It's in the past, and she must move on. I still think if you married first, she'd follow suit."

Evelina frowned. "Fenella is no more a follower than I am. Besides, if I marry first, then she'll see it as a ticket to freedom and spinsterhood. She deserves love as much as I do."

Lady Franklin shook her head and took the chair next to her daughter. "Why couldn't she have been more like you instead of such a clunch?"

She arched a brow, irritated with the comparison. Though Evelina was a more traditional beauty than her sister, Fenella had an ethereal loveliness. They were opposites in personality and physical traits. Evelina had always been friendly and outgoing. Fenella was a bluestocking who had few close friends but fiercely loyal. Evelina was petite and curvy compared to Fenella's tall, litheness. Evelina had hair the color of dark honey, while Fenella's was pale blonde. Her eyes were a light brown, almost amber. Fenella had their father's clear gray eyes.

"Mama, let's be honest. Your true goal is for one of your daughters to marry a titled gentleman—not just find a good match—so you can receive more prestigious invitations. My sister doesn't belong with the *beau monde*." She winced as Louella caught on a knot and worked it out with her fingers. "I have promised to do my best, but there is no changing who we are. Gloriously rich merchants who can buy their way into almost any event in Town. A leopard cannot change his spots and shouldn't have to. Why can you not be happy when we have so much?"

"I am quite satisfied with my life. There is nothing wrong with a baronet, except your father is not a peer. I hate it when those plump, smug women look down their noses at me with a patronizing smile," huffed her mother. "Besides, with your beauty, there is no reason we can't improve our standing. A baron or viscount would be lucky to have such a diamond of the first water."

16

"I suppose we should be thankful you aren't hoping for a duke."

"Oh, gracious. There are so few dukes, even marquesses. An earl, though..."

Evelina sighed. An ember in the hearth popped and drew her attention, her mind wandering as she gazed at the crackling flames. Guilt once again twisted in her chest. She *was* excited for her first season. Unlike Fenella, she loved the attention and new gowns, the flirting and dancing. Since she'd been a girl, she'd had the same dream of her first ball.

The most handsome man in the room, dressed complete to a shade, would bow and ask her to dance. It would be a waltz. His dark hair would gleam under the candlelight of a dozen chandeliers; his hand would rest on her waist, his warm palm against her gloved one. The orchestra would strike the first notes, and she would whirl and spin as her champion held her close, their eyes locked. They would finish the dance, both breathless, and he would escort her outside for a breath of air. On the balcony, or during a stroll through the garden, he would bend his head and lightly touch his lips to hers. A tingle would shoot from her head to her toes, and with just one kiss, she would know it was love.

"Mama, you cannot use us as sacrificial lambs. I will choose the man who wins my heart. I pray for *your* sake that he has a title. I pray for *my* sake that he has a sense of humor when he meets my family." She followed her maid to the bed, dropped her robe, and lifted her arms as Louella helped her don the soft cotton night rail. "Now, I am dreadfully tired. The season doesn't really begin for another month. May we continue this conversation later?"

"Of course, my dear. The modiste comes tomorrow, and it will be a long day for all of us." Lady Franklin kissed her daughter on the forehead and patted her cheek. "Before you ask, I promise to be patient with Fenella during the fittings."

❄

The ice beneath her shining blades reflected her coquelicot red pelisse and matching bonnet. Evelina pulled the leather strap taut and secured it around her ankle. Then she tightened the ribbons of her hat, pulling the wide, flared brim closer to the sides of her face to protect her skin from the chilly breeze. She had added several gold feathers under the band, knowing they would flutter gracefully as she skated.

The Serpentine had frozen, providing a chance to enjoy one last skating session before the winter receded. Hyde Park was filled with Londoners taking advantage of the day. On the north bank of the river, carriages cluttered the side of the road. On the opposite side, groups of pedestrians gathered and watched those brave enough to skate. Most were men, which had never given her pause. The ladies preferred to observe and gossip or venture out for a brief slide with a partner. Evelina would smile sweetly at any disapproving looks from the matrons, then with a slight bow, perform what school boys called a Turk's Cap. The figure entailed cutting the numeral three, thrice, until she connected the numbers and formed the shape of a turban.

"You really should try the blades, Fenella," she urged once more as she glided a circle around her sister. "The steel is much better quality than the old wooden blades we had as children. I can move so fast, it's... exhilarating." She held her arms out and spun again. "Like flying."

"If I had your skill and confidence, I might attempt it. But my lengthy frame sprawled on the ice would only create a scandal. Or seriously hurt someone." Fenella laughed and shuffled a few feet on the soles of her boots. She clutched the lapels of her slate redingote, her knuckles white. "I prefer the saddle. The horse is in charge of balance, and I only need to hold on."

"It takes balance to stay mounted. You could outride me any day."

"That may be, but think of the snickers and whispers if I fell. *You* sprawled on your backside, however, would draw a dozen beaus to your rescue." Fenella's smile did not reach her eyes as she pushed back a pale flaxen curl from her cheek. "Not that I blame them, Evie."

"Nonsense, we are different but complementary! You are willowy and lissome to my, um... compact but graceful athleticism," she finished valiantly, hands on her hips, relieved when their cousin Charles joined them.

"Greetings, lovely ladies, is it not a splendid day?" he asked with a mock bow, at ease and steady on his own skates. "A final gift from Old Man Winter. With these temperatures, tomorrow will be too late to safely swagger and flaunt my prowess."

"Who are you trying to impress today, dear sir?" asked Fenella, nodding to a pair of giggling girls under a tree. "The pretty blonde with the pout or the darkhaired beauty who seems to follow your every move?"

"Both." He grinned, his auburn hair shining red in the afternoon sun. His gray eyes twinkled as glanced over his cousins and noted the taller sister's boots. "You should take more risks," he said with a wink. "Life is a gamble, sweet Fenella, and you can't win if you don't wager."

"I'll keep that in mind when you need another loan," Fenella quipped back. "In the meantime, lend me your arm so I don't make a fool of myself."

"I've already promised both my admirers a promenade around the Serpentine. However, a friend of mine has arrived in London and doesn't know anyone here. Let me introduce you."

Evelina giggled as Charles dashed away before Fenella could protest. He disappeared behind one of the booths pitched to sell refreshments. "He will never understand the art of subtlety, will he?"

"No, he won't," agreed her sister. "I hope he's not trying to… What if—"

"I'm sure the gentleman will be fine if he's a friend. Perhaps he's a longshank and not shorter than you?" she ventured with her usual optimism.

"I can only hope," agreed Fenella. "It's almost worth the legshackles of marriage to avoid this constant parade of *eligible* men. Oh, the expression in their eyes when they look *up* at me."

"One day, a man will look into those gray eyes, brush back your white-gold locks, and declare his undying love for you." Evelina hugged her. "He's out there, somewhere, you know. We just need to find him."

"You really should be on stage," Fenella said but gave her another side hug. "What would I do without you?"

Evie shrugged her shoulders, then spotted her cousin, returning through the colorful display of bright pelisses and fur-trimmed redingotes, bonnets, beaver hats, and elegant great coats. Charles appeared with his friend, a tall, lanky, handsome man with soft brown eyes. His hair was pale blond and combed straight back. In fact, it was almost the exact color of Fenella's long tresses. Evelina watched her sister smile, the tension draining from Fenella's body as she straightened, no longer hiding her height.

"Ladies, may I introduce my good friend, Viscount Raines. My lord, these are my cousins Miss Franklin and Miss Evelina." Charles smiled and nodded at each female as he spoke their names.

"It's my pleasure." Lord Raines executed a perfect leg and bowed. When he stood, he was at least a head taller than Fenella.

Evelina narrowed her eyes, studying the man. "Have we met before, Lord Raines? You seem very familiar."

The viscount shook his head. "I do not believe so, Miss Evelina. My mother enjoyed the season before she married, but alas, my father preferred the country. I am rarely afforded an opportunity to enjoy London's leisure activities."

"Hmm," she murmured, looking between him and her sister. There was something about the man she couldn't quite...

"Would you care to walk, Miss Franklin?" Lord Raines held out his arm.

To Evelina's surprise, Fenella smiled, placed her hand in the crook of his elbow, and slid one foot forward. "I pray, sir, I do not pull us both down when we must cross the ice."

"Never fear. I may not look it, but I'm sturdy as an oak. Lean on me if you feel unstable." The viscount's words faded as they moved away.

With her sister in capable hands, Evelina picked up her skirts and glided to the middle of the frozen circle. She would get a lecture about her chapped cheeks, but it was worth the price. How she loved the outdoors. Days like this were a gift, and a girl was mad not to take advantage.

She skated the perimeter of the Serpentine, leaning right, then left, turning about, and continuing backwards. With her eyes closed, she listened to the *sssssk* of the steel against the frozen river. She slowed near the end of the skating area, twisted, and turned to move forward again. Ahead of her, Lord Raines and her sister moved slowly along the bank. What a fortuitous meeting. She hoped they were getting along well.

With a splash of pulverized ice, she stopped beside them. "You didn't fall, I hope?" she asked, biting her lip.

"No, I did not. My lord was not exaggerating when he said he was solid as an oak. He's been thoroughly tested and approved." She rubbed her gloves together. "I am ready for a bit of warmth, though. The sun is already moving to the west, and I'm feeling the chill."

"Shall we rest and share a cup of saloop?" ventured Lord Raines.

"Oh, yes," agreed Evelina, thinking of the tasty sassafras tea. "Let me take my blades off."

Charles joined them just as the trio headed toward one of the vendors. "I say, it's been a splendid day." He winked at Fenella. "Did my friend treat you well?"

"Abominably," she answered with a grin. "However did you find a male in London who enjoys an intelligent conversation?"

"If your cousin wasn't such a beauty, I'd take offense," said the viscount in mock horror. They stopped at the wheeled cart. "It seems we both enjoy a balanced ledger and have similar interests in estate management."

"I'm glad to hear it, and gladder still I wasn't part of the conversation." Charles ordered four bowls of the steaming tea. "I did warn you, though!"

A plump woman dressed in several layers, a mob cap and bonnet, and fingerless gloves sat next to the portable table. Bowls were stacked next to her elbow, and she pushed the lever on the samovar's spout and filled a dish. Passing the first to Fenella, the licorice scent wafted under Evelina's nose. She accepted the second bowl and wrapped her gloves around the warmth. A strange sense of being watched made her peer over her shoulder. Some pedestrians, a few gentlemen on horseback, but no one familiar or beckoning to her.

A horse whinnied and a tall, darkhaired man moved away from the walking path. He was dressed fashionably in breeches and Hessians, his black greatcoat expensively tailored. As he urged his mount by the vendor, their gaze met. A hundred butterflies battered her insides, and one hand pressed against the stomach to stop the wings. The man was incredibly handsome with a trimmed beard and piercing brown eyes. No, green. Like emerald ice chips embedded in a circle of amber. The stranger gave a slight nod, the corner of his full lips almost tipping in a smile. She drew in air, not realizing she'd been holding her breath.

"There's milk and sugar, if you prefer, my ladies," the vendor said, nodding to a tin and a small pitcher, and pulling Evelina back to the moment. "Me husband's selling roasted chestnuts over there for those with a taste."

When she turned back, the man was gone. She shook her head, scoffing at the strange hollowness that had replaced the flutter in her belly. The group finished their saloop and wound their way through the thinning crowd. Orange and red streaked the sky as the girls stepped into their waiting carriage. "Thank you for a lovely afternoon," Fenella said to the men. "Perhaps we'll meet again, Lord Raines."

"I hope so, ladies, but I doubt if it will be soon. I head north tomorrow, back to my estate. I do, however, come to London several times a year." He doffed his hat, the late afternoon rays brightening his blond crown. "I shall call on Charles when I return."

As soon as their conveyance lurched forward, Evelina pounced. "He seemed quite taken with you."

Fenella sniffed. "He is a very nice man and takes care of his invalid mother. His father died a year ago, and he's spent the past months learning the estate. We had a wonderful conversation about breeding sheep and—"

"All the things Mama warned you against," Evelina interrupted with a laugh. "But did you like him?"

"I do, but as a fine man who engages in lively and witty conversation, not as a suitor."

"No flutter?"

"Not even a pit-a-pat." Fenella gave her sister a side glance. "He thought you were quite beautiful."

"Pish and petunias! He's much too fair for me. You know I prefer the dark, mysterious type."

"Promise me something," Fenella said, squeezing Evelina's hand.

"Anything."

"If you do meet this dark, handsome, mysterious man and I'm not yet married, promise me you won't let him pass you by." Fenella chewed her lip but held Evie's gaze. "I would never forgive myself if you lost your chance at love because I'm too…"

"I promise, under one condition."

"Does there always have to be a bargain?" Fenella laughed and blinked, her gray eyes bright.

Evelina hated seeing the unshed tears, wanted to provide comfort and assurance that all would be well. It wasn't fair that one of them had the features admired by society and the other a more distinctive beauty. Her sister was a prime article, just underappreciated. Evelina swallowed the lump in her throat.

"I'm a Franklin, aren't I? I promise if Cupid's arrow finds me first, I will not duck. But you must do the same." She cupped Fenella's cheek in her palm and forced a cheery smile. "As Lord Raines proved today, there are good, decent —and handsome—men. And one of them will be honored to have you as a wife. Swear to me that you will keep your heart open when that time comes."

"Agreed. Now we only have to find the elusive man who will suit one of us *and* have the title Mama covets." Fenella leaned back against the velvet squab with a sigh.

Evelina snorted. "I suppose we could promise our first born."

CHAPTER THREE

February 1819
Brecken Castle, Wales

*M*adoc closed his eyes, slammed the ledger shut, and let out his breath. A long, ragged, resigned breath. Brecknock and its adjoining lands had always been self-sufficient. Fields were set aside and rotated for human and livestock consumption, meat and dairy animals were kept, tradesmen resided in the village. But the crops and beef cattle had been sold and not replaced, with all profits going to the estate manager. No winter turnips or potatoes had been planted to help the tenants through till the next harvest.

The estate was on the rocks, his father taken ill, and they didn't have a sixpence to scratch with.

Caerton had paid a visit the morning of Madoc's return. The steward had informed Lord Brecken that he'd received a lucrative opportunity elsewhere and was putting in his notice. The earl had gone into a rampage, which had both thrilled and horrified Lady Brecken. Thrilled he was speaking and taking an interest in his surroundings. Horrified at the anger and threats that echoed loudly down the hall. The chancer fled the next day when news had spread of Lord Madoc's arrival. Charges had been filed, but there was little else to do. For now. "I'll find you, Niall, you bloody devil. You'll pay one way or another."

In the meantime, the tenants were in a bad way. He had put the men to work repairing homes and vital shops. Griff, his half-brother from his mother's first marriage, had sent grain and other staples from Monmouth. It had galled Madoc to ask for help, but at least he had family to turn to. His parents needed to understand the dire circumstances they now faced.

He pushed away from the desk and found them in the library, seated by the hearth. Lord Brecken's chin hung low, and he snored lightly. His mother smiled as Madoc leaned against the mantel. She had aged since he'd been gone. Silver threaded her dark hair, but her eyes remained clear and alert. He remembered a time when she had been his world. Her laughter had reminded him of delicate crystal bells, and he'd been certain no one could equal her beauty. Mama had doted on him, spent time with him, and listened to him until her husband's infirmity had consumed her.

"How was your day, son?" she asked and patted the seat next to her on the chaise longue.

He sat next to her and studied the sleeping form. Last month, he'd returned to find his father in a rage and his mother at sixes and sevens. Lady Brecken had met him at the door in tears, insisting the earl had gone mad.

The scene was forever etched in his mind. An old man stood gripping the mantel, ranting to have his horse brought round. An old woman begging him to be reasonable, that he wasn't able to walk, let alone ride. But Brecken *had* tried to walk, bellowing at his wife to shut up and obey him. Lord Brecken had returned until he fell face first on the floor. Madoc and the countess had watched in horror as a scarlet puddle seeped from the earl's head and stained the carpet. Madoc had carried the unconscious form to his chamber, a sobbing mother following him up the two flights of stairs.

The physician had guaranteed the earl's skull would heal from the concussion but could not predict whether the patient would wake from the injury or to his state of mind. What if the silent brooding father he'd left became a babbling incompetent? The worst scenario would be an endless sleep, his mother hovering over a prone form until he took his last breath.

Guilt twisted in his gut. Could he have stopped the course of events leading to this? If he'd been home, would Caerton have succeeded in bleeding the estate? A low growl scratched at his throat. *What ifs* and hindsight weren't viable solutions.

"I have some funds to get us by for now, but this is a large estate. The roofs are repaired and grain purchased, so we're good until spring." He ran a hand through his hair. "We'll need to find a way to produce more income until it's functioning and making a profit again. I have no idea where to begin."

"Once your father wakes up, he'll know what to do." She patted Madoc's hand. "He loves you, you know, and will appreciate all you've done."

"Blast, Mama, we don't know if he'll ever be cognizant again." He stood and walked to the side table, pouring a whisky. What he wouldn't give for some fine Cognac right now. "I've prioritized the most urgent issues, and we'll work our way down the list."

"Mind your tongue. I'm still your mother." She wagged a finger at her son. "Is there nothing left?"

"I apologize, and yes, we still have the property. Every bit of coin, anything Caerton had the authority to sell, he did. He scraped every morsel of flesh from the carcass before he made his escape." He threw back the whisky and winced as it burned his throat. "I need brandy, not this blasted fire water."

"Getting foxed won't help us."

"Nor is waiting for Father to wake up and make everything better." He clenched his jaw and looked up to the ceiling, studying the intricate plaster crown molding. *Patience!* "I'm sorry, Mama, truly I am. This is just so galling."

"I understand." She pressed her lips together and squeezed her eyes shut. "It's only that... he's such a magnificent man. Even now when he wraps his arms around me, it's like the world melted away. Nothing can harm me. Nothing can touch me."

"He adores you. Always has."

Lady Brecken nodded and dabbed at her eyes with a handkerchief. "My first marriage was arranged by my father. I was a dutiful wife and gave my first husband the expected heir, so fate rewarded me. As a young widow, *I* chose my next husband."

"How did you meet?"

She laughed. "A foxhunt, of course. A mutual friend invited me to a country party. Two weeks of glorious distraction from the worries of a baby and horrid mother-in-law. I was a carefree girl again. Then Lord Brecken rode in from the field on his enormous white steed, and I caught his eye. He bowed to me from the saddle and..." Her voice faded, a slight smile curving her lips, and he knew she was conjuring the details of that first encounter.

"You knew right away?" Madoc always scoffed at the female ideology of love at first sight.

"No. I had just endured a year of mourning and a woman who despised me for outliving her son. She was threatening to keep *my* son if I remarried." She smiled at her sleeping husband. "But when Brecken looked at me and bellowed, 'Who brought this stunning creature? I've been looking for her all my life.' I realized my life had finally begun. Every time I turned around that first few days, he was there with a refreshment, or a compliment, or a request. He proposed the following week, before the first guest had departed. I said yes without hesitation."

"No regrets? Not even now?"

"Love, genuine love, doesn't diminish or become a hardship. It's what keeps me going, gets me out of bed in the morning, convinces me to look my best. So I'm still the sweet Maggie he calls for to give him a kiss. Our hearts still touch, although it's a different kind of love now but as powerful." Her voice broke. "So no, I have no regrets. He's made my life worth living, and I'll be by his side until the end. Whenever that may be."

As she spoke, her features soft and her dark eyes shining, Madoc could see the young girl she'd been. An ache in his chest made him reach out to her, and he held his mother for the first time in years. She was once again the caring, beautiful Mama he'd known as a child, who loved her son as much as she loved her husband. The woman she'd been before his father's accident, before their lives had all tumbled over that hedge.

"Doc! Oh heavens, Doc!"

Madoc set down his tea and brushed a few crumbs off his waistcoat. His mother's urgent tone made him quit his breakfast. With long, hurried strides, he took the steps two at a time and stopped outside the bed chamber. *What the devil was going on?*

"Good morning, son. Maggie just told me you've come home. I'm sorry I wasn't more fit when you arrived." His father, propped up against the bolsters, held out his hand to shake his son's. "I want to hear about your travels."

His mother hurried to the door. "I told you he'd come back to us." Her eyes shone with hope. "I'll have tea brought in here and give the two of you some time alone."

Madoc could only nod as he moved past her to sit across from his father. It was like he'd come back from the dead. His voice was weak, but held the same confident, jovial tone of years past. Green sparkled against the golden brown in his eyes, and a smile took ten years off his creased face.

"It's good to see you so... awake, Father. We've missed you."

The bushy gray brows furrowed, then relaxed. "Well, tell me about Egypt. Did you see the pyramids? And India? I remember my Grand Tour."

The two men chatted and laughed for an hour. Madoc remained vague about his own travels and would say just enough to draw the earl into a story and sit back to listen. It had been so long since he'd heard his father recount an adventure. The old man hadn't lost his touch.

"Enough reminiscing," barked Brecken. "What's going on with the estate? Maggie says there's trouble. By God, where's Caerton?"

Madoc hesitated, wondering if this would put his father over the edge again. "Which Caerton?" he asked, carefully feeling his way.

"Niall, of course. Didn't you hear?" Brecken's eyes narrowed. "Or are you testing me?"

He chuckled at his father's insight. The man had a right to know the condition of his own holdings, so he gave a brief summary.

"It can't be as bad as that."

"Perhaps you need to see it for yourself." It was an unseasonably warm day. They could bring the carriage around—

"Splendid idea. Some fresh air would be just the thing." Brecken tossed off his blanket and slapped his thigh. "Don't tell your mother. She's busy with the week's menu and would worry too much. Call for my valet and a couple footmen."

An hour later, the Earl of Brecken and his son rumbled down a lane toward Brecknock. The sun glinted off the layer of frost still covering the ground. Fluffy white clouds hung above them in a cornflower blue sky. The air was crisp but not biting as the earl opened a shutter and tipped his head out the window to inhale a deep breath. Dressed in a bottle-green waistcoat, fawn trousers, and a perfectly tied cravat, it was as if time had spun backwards.

"I feel like I've been in deep sleep, and the world has changed while I've been gone." His eyes narrowed when they passed the dormant fields and some bony dairy cows. "Where's the livestock?"

"Sold."

Anger sparked in his eyes, his fists bunched, as they passed by dilapidated barns and hungry dairy cows. When he saw some of the tenants he'd known since a boy, thin and underdressed for the winter, he exploded. "What kind of monster lets his own people suffer? Caerton was part of this town, worked with these men, celebrated holidays with these families. By God, he'll pay for this."

Word spread quickly that the master was up and about. Madoc had always known his father was popular and well-liked, but this welcome surprised him. By the time the carriage reached the end of the main street, a crowd had gathered at the small square. Children jumped up and down to see inside the fancy coach. Adults waved and smiled, relief and hope brightening their faces.

"God bless you, my lord," one woman yelled.

"We knew you'd come round," cried another.

The earl ordered the carriage to stop.

Lord Brecken waved to the crowd. "I'm afraid I've been amiss in my duties. If I'd known what was happening, but my... condition. I can only thank you for not leaving." His voice broke. "I will right the wrongs done to you. I give you my word, my son and I will restore these lands."

"Lord Madoc already had my roof re-thatched," called one man. "And he's sent us grain, so our babes have bread to eat, and our livestock won't starve."

An elderly man stepped forward, his homespun shirt and coat threadbare at the elbows and cuffs. He doffed his cap and stared at his worn leather boots as he spoke. "After sixty some years on this earth, and living off this soil—this partic- ular soil—I wouldn't leave because of four bad ones." The man grinned, exposing several missing teeth, and looked the earl in the eye. "This is our home, my lord. Where else would we be? Loyalty goes both ways between us. The name Brecken has always been respected as noblemen who kept their word."

The blacksmith stepped forward. "Aye, my lord, and the young master will follow in your footsteps. We have no doubt."

"Thank you, for your allegiance *and* your honesty."

The earl's face paled, and panic surged through Madoc. "Now it's time to go home, Father."

The silence on the ride home weighed on them both. One thinking of mistakes made in the past, the other pondering the future. A wheel hit a rut and jostled them against the leather squabs, causing both men to reach for the leather arm straps. The sorrow and regret in his father's eyes tore at Madoc's heart. He wanted to solve this problem for his parents but was at a loss, except to sell off part of the land.

There were several smaller holdings that could be let go. He mentioned this and was astonished at the quick response.

"Whatever we need to do, Doc. It's not about the coin, not now. Those fine, hard-working people have always depended on us. It took generations to build the trust we have and my stubbornness might have washed us all down the river. Their lives, Maggie's future, your inheritance." Brecken ran a hand over his face and rubbed his jaw. "I let my own misfortune become their misfortune. I let my pride rob me of ten years of happiness and... living. Hound's teeth, but I need to repair the damage done."

"I'm here to help, Father. We'll figure this out together." He leaned over and squeezed his father's arm. "Whatever happens, at least you're alive and of sound mind again."

Brecken nodded, wiped his eyes with his palms, and whispered, "You're a good son."

Lady Brecken met them in the courtyard just as Madoc was opening the carriage door, worry deepening the lines around her eyes. "Don't you ever sneak out like that again! I'll, I'll—"

"Kiss me, Maggie."

Her eyes glistened as she placed a foot on the step and leaned inside the coach. She placed her lips to his, then pulled back, blushing.

He stroked her pink cheek. "There's never been anything more precious, my sweeting."

"I love you, even if you are a cantankerous, arrogant, handsome, infuriating oaf!" She moved aside for the footmen to help the earl inside, not bothering to hide her very improper grin. "Take him upstairs, please. We'll take a light supper in our rooms."

Late February
   London, England

Madoc let out a long breath and pulled his horse to a stop near the Serpentine. It was done. Two properties sold, half the money safely set aside for the estate and the other half invested. He'd met up with an old army comrade Kit, the Earl of Sunderland, for some much-needed advice. After explaining his dilemma, Kit had invited him to join in the purchase of a textile mill near Manchester. This was the second declining factory that Sunderland had financed. The first made a profit within a year.

"Doc, you need an income until the estate is self-sufficient again. A few wise financial ventures could get you out of low water. Give you the coin you need to make the repairs, then build from there."

"I can't justify spending money when we need it so desperately." Madoc had thrown back the last gulp of claret. *"But I admit, I'm at a loss."*

"If you must sell property, be sensible about it. By investing half the profit, the estate will have a steady income in another year or so. It will keep you afloat after your cash has run out." Kit poured them both another glass and grinned. *"And I've sent a cask of fine French brandy to Brecken Castle. I recall mentioning your father only keeps that godawful whisky stocked. Consider it a donation to the cause."*

Hyde Park was busy for a winter afternoon. The river had frozen, and there were skaters on the Serpentine. He found himself with a fit of the blue-devils, as if he'd failed in some way by selling off a couple holdings he'd never even seen.

Without thinking, he'd guided the horse to Rotten Row and found himself wandering the park. Laughter echoed across the ice, and he stopped under a tree to watch the activity. He stood in the stirrups to see over the row of conveyances and his eyes fell on a swirling red pelisse. Honey-brown hair fluttered beneath her bonnet, mimicking the feathers atop her bonnet. She was graceful and unabashed, enjoying herself immensely if one judged by the beguiling smile curving her lips.

Madoc settled back into the saddle and squeezed the gelding's flanks, moving closer to the carriages. He wanted—no needed—to gaze at this lovely creature if only for a while. His eyes followed her as she glided past, not losing sight of the flash of scarlet that darted between other skaters and pedestrians. A chuckle rumbled in his chest as she turned and continued backward, her head tipped down. He lost track of time as he watched her petite form sashay back and forth, keeping rhythm to some tune only she could hear. The longer he watched her, the more buoyant his mood. Something about her called to him, a whisper of enticement that tickled his soul.

"Thank you for leading your preoccupied master here," he said to the bay gelding, patting its sleek, muscular neck as he urged him forward. "Just what I needed today."

The woman stopped to talk to another couple, then another gentleman joined them. His features were similar to the tall, elegant blonde standing next to the prime article he'd been admiring. The foursome moved toward the stall selling hot drinks. Madoc watched her movements, the expression in her cognac eyes. *Stunning* was the first word that came to mind. He resisted the urge to dismount and wander closer. When she brought a dish to her mouth, he groaned. Her profile showed a pert nose and full lips. She had a woman's curves, though she appeared young. Then she stiffened and turned toward him. Had she felt him watching her?

Her gaze locked with his. Blood rushed through his veins, heat simmered and pooled low in his belly. For a moment, he could understand Kit's impassioned words about his wife. Never had a woman cast such a spell on him. He nodded, almost smiled but caught himself, then pulled his horse away from the revelers.

With a swift kick, he sent them into a trot, away from the skating goddess and back to his hotel. Back to Wales and his parents. This time, he would leave London with a lighter heart. His father had remained lucid, and his mother was once again the mama he'd loved as a child. It had been as if the return of the earl had brought her back to life as well.

The path ahead of him—restoring the lands and finding a trustworthy steward—would be difficult and no doubt fraught with setbacks. Yet, his outlook was so much sunnier than only a month ago. Who knew what tomorrow would bring?

CHAPTER FOUR

March 1819
Brecken Castle

*A*nxiety niggled at Madoc as he unbuttoned his waistcoat and pulled off his linen shirt. He was bone-tired, and his bed was calling his name. He'd been home only a few days and found his father's physical health once again failing, though his mind and humor were still intact. This kept Lady Brecken hopeful, but Madoc resigned himself to the inevitable. The earl was dying.

At dawn, he woke to intense pounding at his door. "My lord, your mother sent me," called a manservant from the hall. "It's your father."

Madoc's pulse raced as he pulled on trousers and a fresh shirt over his head. He ran his fingers through mussed hair as he strode down the hall. Inside the earl's rooms, the earl lay propped up against bolsters, his skin a dull gray against the white linen nightshirt.

"What happened? Did you send for the physician?" he asked, gripping one of the bed posts.

His mother nodded. She still wore her night clothes and an ivory velvet dressing gown. "He woke me an hour ago, clutching his chest. I'm so glad he's resting now."

"His heart, you think?" Was he to blame? Had the neglect the earl witnessed been too heavy a burden? Madoc fought the rising panic and the urge to blame himself.

"He said the pain began in his chest, like a slow-burning explosion. I held him, but there was little else I could do. Then he collapsed, and I thought—" She bit down on her fist to hold back a sob and turned for the door. "I'll have some lavender water brought up. It might soothe him."

"Doc." His father's voice was thready, and his eyes remained closed.

"I'm here," he said, leaning over the prone form and taking the chilled leathery hand.

"Don't let your pride keep you from living the life. Every breath is a gift, and I've wasted the last ten years of it." He gripped Madoc's hand, the old man's yellowed nails digging into the smooth, younger flesh of his son. After several short breaths, he continued, "Make amends for me, Madoc, with the tenants. Set the estate to rights again, if you can, and then live. Live your life with no regrets."

Madoc nodded, his eyes burning. He blinked, holding back the emotions that roiled through him. The memories of a father he had idolized as a youth. A time when the Earl of Brecken had seemed invincible.

"Promise," he growled, his lids opening and pinning his son with a hard glare.

"Yes, Father, I swear." With his free hand, Madoc covered the top of his father's and squeezed, feeling the elder's grip relax after the oath was given.

"Tell your mother... Tell her..."

A *woosh* of skirts, and she appeared next to the bed. "Yes, my love." Her dark eyes shone with tears and a tremulous smile curved her lips. "I'm here." Settling next to him on the mattress, she gathered his fingers and cradled his palm against her cheek.

"Don't cry over me, *fy annwyl*," he whispered, using his familiar Welsh endearment for her. "Be happy for me. I'll be whole again soon."

"I'd rather have you with me. You've only just returned to me."

"I'll always be here, watching over you. We both knew with our age difference that I'd go long before you." The earl managed a tired smile while his thumb stroked her skin gently. "You're still the most beautiful woman I've ever known. Our wedding day was the happiest day of my life. I never understood why you chose an old man like me when you could have had your pick of young dandies."

She looked up, a tangle of black curls clinging to her tear-streaked face. "You were my knight in shining armor, so gallant and strong. You swept me off my feet, and my heart was lost."

A sob escaped her, and she fell across his chest, tears soaking his nightshirt. "You cannot leave me. Not yet, not now. We haven't had nearly enough time."

"And I'm afraid I've wasted the last ten years." He paused, eyes closed as he drew in a ragged breath. "I'm truly sorry. My ego stole so much from us. Forgive me."

Madoc watched his parents, witnessed the deep love they had for one another. He swallowed, his throat thick, realizing how lonely his mother must have been. Never had she left his side since the day of the accident. Guilt twisted in his gut.

Images flashed across his mind. Memories of teasing and laughing, the stolen kisses and shared, knowing looks between his parents that had been so frequent. His own childhood had been happy and carefree, doted on by the earl and countess and most of the staff. His father, a barrel-chested man, had maintained his physical strength into his fifties. He could outride and outshoot any man in the county of Brecknock. The earl was known for a ready smile, a quick frown, and a booming laugh or reprimand. Madoc had strived to emulate his father in everything.

Until the accident. He and his mother had tried patience, funny stories, visits from old friends, every remedy they could think of—even threats—to pull him from his self-pity and depression. Nothing had worked. How was he to know catastrophe would be the key to unlock his closed mind and bitter heart? Bollocks! Why did this family have such a tendency for extremes?

Madoc backed slowly from the room, leaving his parents alone for their final goodbyes. For he knew with a grave certainty that the earl would be dead before the day ended. He'd seen enough death over the years to know when a man was near his last breath. His mind whirled with the complications of his father's imminent death, and he willed his mind to focus amid the grief that threatened to break his composure. He'd planned on more time to get reacquainted with the estate, gain the trust of the tenants.

The physician would be here soon. There would be arrangements to make and correspondence... He returned to his rooms and finished dressing. When he entered the library, the decanter of brandy glittered in the morning sun. Madoc didn't think twice.

"Thank you, Kit," he said to the ceiling as he poured the amber liquid. "I'll need some liquid fortitude to get me through this day."

The funeral was simple and heartfelt. The villagers came out in their Sunday best to wave farewell to a master who had treated them well. Their eyes still haunted Madoc—the doubt, the hope, the unasked questions he couldn't yet answer.

He leaned back in his father's overstuffed leather chair and stared at the letter. One week of mourning, and the Home Office needed him back in London. His mother would have an apoplexy.

The conspirators he'd tracked from America to France and back to England, active members of the Spencean Philanthropists, had made contact with a nobleman. Why would the Duke of Colvin, one of the oldest and most respected families in England, have connections to known radicals? Madoc rubbed his jaw, mentally moving around pieces of the puzzle. His man Walters, an ex-Bow Street runner, was keeping an eye on the trio and would give Madoc a full report when he returned to Town. Walters was also trying to locate Caerton, though the scoundrel was likely out of the country by now.

"Well, no time like the present," he said to himself and pushed away from the massive oak desk. Tiny snowflakes fell from an iron-gray sky and pelted the windowpanes. Winter was reluctant to loosen its hold on the land. The day reflected his mood, he thought with a grunt.

Lady Brecken was in the sitting room, a large square of embroidery in her lap. The large brocade wing-back chair seemed to swallow her petite frame. Her eyes gazed out the window, fixed on the white specks swirling against the glass. She startled when her son entered the room. When had she become so fragile?

"Mama, I'm glad I found you." He leaned against the mantel, studying the life-size portrait of his father. Dressed in riding clothes, dark hair smoothed back under the tall beaver hat, fox hounds at his feet and horse at his shoulder, it was hard to imagine such vitality gone. Madoc was now the Earl of Brecken and uncomfortable with his new title.

"You're a younger version of him, you know." Her eyes narrowed as she studied her son. "What has you worried? Is there something I can do?"

"Only by not berating me for leaving so soon." He sighed and turned back to her. "I've business in London."

She poked the needle into the fine linen material and set her embroidery aside. "I'll admit the timing is not ideal. However, the season is beginning in Town. You should think about marriage."

"Mama, please, I've just inherited a failing estate." He sank onto the chair facing her. "I've enough obligations right now without taking on—"

"Exactly my point. A generous dowry could make your life much easier." Lady Brecken pursed her lips. "Doc, I've taken stock of the immediate grounds this past week. I had no idea how badly the buildings and garden deteriorated. We need money."

"I'm doing everything I can."

"Not everything. As the earl, you also need sons. A wealthy wife could give us financial security and, of course, an heir. I won't remind you of our promise to your father."

His brows furrowed at her sharp tone. "I'm aware of my commitments and responsibilities. I'm also cognizant of the fact I have nothing to offer in return. Marriage is a bargain where both parties benefit."

"Nonsense. This earldom goes back to Henry VII, *and* you're young and handsome. Many girls could do much worse. If we're lucky, there might be a knight, lavishly rewarded by the crown, with a daughter of marriageable age. As a last resort, a successful merchant would be ecstatic to have his family connected to ours. We're far from London, so it won't matter to the locals if her father lacks a title." His mother rose. "I won't rest until we've restored Brecken Castle and its holdings to its former glory."

Madoc swore softly as his mother stormed past him, her eyes bright with tears. We? What blasted help would *she* be, except to harass him now to accept the parson's trap? His future now hovered over him like a storm cloud, dark and menacing. What kind of female would marry a penniless earl, agree to life so far removed from society, and live in a dilapidated castle? Not one with a face he'd want to wake up and gaze upon each morning.

He reached for his brandy.

Late March

How the devil had he gone from a spy for His Majesty's government to a sacrificial lamb? He hated this place, with its lemonade and thin, delicate finger sandwiches that would never fill a man's stomach. Yet, here he stood in breeches instead of his usual trousers, on parade for all the simpering mamas and the silly, bird-witted girls. A cluster of females giggled under the musicians' balcony, casting glances about the room and settling on him. *I feel like a new hat in a shop window*, he thought as he leaned against one of Almack's white plaster pillars.

His mother had been correct, though. The patronesses had sent a voucher upon request. The infamous marriage mart now greeted him with enthusiasm. One visit to these infamous halls, and he was ready to sign on for the next war. Perhaps he'd start one. In the meantime, he shared the misery of several female wallflowers trying to blend into the woodwork. Madoc squinted at a tall blonde in a sea-green dress, attempting to hide behind a flimsy plant. He chuckled at her effort. Until she was joined by another petite lady with soft brown curls.

His heart jolted.

It was the skating goddess from Hyde Park. He'd put her out of his mind since his last trip to Town. She was dressed in a pale pink silk, with capped sleeves giving way to creamy shoulders and a hint of cleavage. Her caramel hair was swept up, paste gems twinkling from the light of the wall sconce. Wispy ringlets framed her heart-shaped face.

Simply exquisite, he thought as she took the long-legged blonde by the hand and pulled her away from the wall. Madoc realized that woman had also been one of the party on the Serpentine. As if sensing his attention, the smaller woman turned to look over her shoulder and caught his eye. Madoc held his breath. Those toffee-color orbs held him in a trance. The sounds around him muffled, and everything around him moved slower as they drank each other in. It could have been a moment or five.

He stepped forward, eager to make her acquaintance, then stopped. *Don't be a green-boy. You've never been introduced,* he scolded himself. In that fleeting moment, she disappeared. *Blast!*

Disappointment swelled in his gut. An unfamiliar sensation when it came to women. He'd find her if it took all evening. What was her family background? Where was the walking Debrett's to answer his questions? He couldn't be fortunate enough to find a woman who both stirred his desire and had the wealth he so desperately needed. His selection for the future Countess of Brecken had been slim to this point. Not that there weren't beauties available. Only none with the kind of dowry he required *and* desperate to marry an earl with empty pockets. It was a tightrope, to be sure. Inquiring into the size of a lady's dowry without revealing he was in Dunn territory. To this end, he'd found the older brother of a military friend, who was happy to recite the appropriate page of Debrett's for any young lady who crossed their path.

"Lord Brooks." He nodded at the short, pretentious baron who joined him. His *social informant,* as he'd begun to think of his new friend, had dull brown hair and eyes. His tongue darted out nervously whenever in conversation with a female, making his thin lips red and shiny after a long evening. To make up for his lack of physical attraction, the man wore enough lace and jewelry for three. He fiddled with a diamond stick pin placed precisely in the center of an enormous intricate cravat that would make Beau Brummel proud.

"Lord Brecken, why are you not dancing? It's why you've come, is it not?"

"No, I did not come for quadrilles or waltzes. I came for a wife. I'd prefer to know she's a possible match before I resign myself to a thirty-minute dance set." Madoc searched the crowd, ignoring the ludicrous commotion in his belly. "And the sooner I achieve success, the sooner I can leave."

"I, for one, will miss you when you're gone. I'm much more popular with a fine-looking earl next to me. And for that, I thank you."

"I'm happy to oblige. Without your assistance, my search could have been endless. Your knowledge of these families is astounding."

"It's ironic, you know," Brooks said, looking up at his companion. "You're here to make the longest commitment of your life, and you're worried about the length of a dance set." The man smiled, showing crooked, butter-colored teeth.

Madoc let out a loud guffaw, causing a couple on promenade to glance their way. "Point made, my friend. Point made." The popinjay was growing on him. He appreciated Brooks' dry wit and quiet commentary. It made these engagements bearable. Four in a week. Did no one ever spend a quiet evening at home in London?

"I'm in the mood for a bit of gaming tonight. Would you care to join me after this?"

"It will give me something to look forward to. This evening has been interminable."

"I promised Lady Franklin that I would dance with her daughter. Then my obligations are complete." Lord Brooks pointed out a young woman wearing a gold atrocity that hugged her ample curves and too many feathers bouncing in her hair. "For now, I'll tell you about that darkhaired bit of muslin. Not the brightest star in the sky, but her father is a banker. He's put out of the word he'd be very generous to any gentleman of good standing who shows an interest."

Madoc studied the woman. She laughed, a garish sound that grated on his nerves. Her eyes were large but too far apart. He couldn't decide if he'd look at one, then the other, or look above her nose and not choose. When the lady cackled again, he mentally struck her name off his list. He could accept a plain wife, but that noise would drive him to lunacy. *Mama would chew her up and spit her out.*

With a sigh, he watched Brooks approach the tall wallflower who had tried to hide behind a potted plant. Though his friend's eye level was even with the woman's chin, he was undaunted by the height difference. Madoc grinned. This would be entertaining.

I promised Lady Franklin that I would dance with her daughter.

Lord Brooks knew a Lady Franklin and was about to dance with her daughter. Her daughter knew the honey-haired goddess. Madoc focused on the couple, determined to be introduced to the mystery woman.

Brooks bowed slightly and engaged Miss Franklin in conversation, his face pleasant and bland. She nodded her head to something he said, then hitched her shoulder up and bent her head as if she had a spasm in her neck. Then her mouth opened; her tongue shot out like a feral adder and made a wide swipe around her lips.

Madoc's mouth dropped open. What in blue blazes was the chit doing? The expression of his friend's face was uproarious, and Doc struggled not to laugh out loud. The hussy chewed on her bottom lip as if there were a bit of beef stuck to it. The baron placed one foot behind him.

He's in retreat, and I don't blame him. Dashed bad timing, though. How would he get an introduction to Miss Franklin's friend?

CHAPTER FIVE

*E*velina watched her sister wage a comical war with the unsuspecting Lord Brooks. Poor man. Though he wasn't handsome, the baron was a nice person, and Evie liked him. She moved to Fenella's side in time to see Lord Brooks' retreat, and their mother headed toward them, her deep brown eyes narrowed and mouth pinched.

"I'll intercept her for you, but what were you thinking?" she asked, waving her fan to cool her cheeks. "You looked like Nora the cow when we put honey on her lips."

Fenella laughed. "I'd forgotten all about that. Well, good. It had the desired effect, then." She picked up her skirt and made a dash for the refreshment table.

"I'll find a way for you to settle this debt," Evie called after her good-naturedly, blocking Lady Franklin's path to her oldest daughter. "Mother, why is your face so mottled? Gracious, let's get you some fresh air. It's stifling in here!"

They walked out of the ballroom and toward a large open window, shutters pushed to display the twinkle of a thousand stars in the midnight sky. A crescent moon shone yellow-white against the inky black. Muffled voices and music followed them. Evelina inhaled the crisp night air, waiting for her mother's tirade.

"Why does she do her best to vex me?" Lady Franklin's jaw tensed as she spoke. She blinked and smoothed the skirt of her slate gray gown. "I only want what's best for her."

"I know that, and you know that, Mama," she agreed. "But Fenella only sees your disapproval and what she lacks in the eyes of others. She's convinced you favor me."

"How can you say that? Why would I try so hard if I didn't love her?" Her mother gripped Evie's arm. "Who else saw that ridiculous performance, do you think?"

Evelina started to sympathize with her mother until the last question. "It doesn't matter, Mama. What matters is my sister is obviously unhappy. We need to find a way to alter that."

"I suppose you have an idea? Please don't say a convent."

A giggle bubbled up Evelina's throat. "Of course not! We're not even Catholic."

"I fear it would be easier to convert my oldest daughter than find her a husband."

Evelina shook her head and hooked her mother's arm with her own. Lord Raines face came to mind, and she smiled. "Let me think on it. I may have an idea. In the meantime, at least send taller men her way."

"I'll try, but choices are slim after last year and her constant attempt this season to put off any man who smiles in her direction."

They re-entered the crowded ballroom, and the heavy warm air smacked her in the face. Pish and posh, it was only March. What would Almack's be like in June? The odor of too many people assembled in one space assaulted her nostrils again. Snapping open her fan, she wafted it under her nose and perused the crowd. She spied Fenella by the refreshment table.

Evelina's breath caught. Standing next to her was the gentleman she'd seen while pulling her sister from hiding earlier.

"You look flushed, my dear. Are you all right?" asked her mother.

Evelina nodded. "I need something cool to drink." She'd apologize to Fenella later for dragging their mother back, but for the love of petunias, she wanted to meet that man.

When their eyes had met, the moment had been dream-like. Her heart raced again, remembering the heat that had swept through her when their gazes locked. One hand cradled her stomach as she walked, but the pesky wings continued to flap.

They weaved their way among the attendees. She saw Lord Brooks approach her sister and the stranger with a wary look. It appeared introductions were made, then the unknown gentleman bowed and kissed Fenella's gloved hand. His broad shoulders strained the well-tailored coat as he bent, then straightened. His smile was heart-stopping, the dark mustache making his teeth appear as white as new snow. He nodded at the baron who escaped with a look of relief. When her sister grinned, Evie's heart sank.

Don't be a wet goose, she scolded herself, *you don't even know the man.* If he was interested in Fenella, she should be ecstatic for her sister. Forcing a smile, they approached the refreshment table. Guilt now batted the butterflies into submission.

"Fenella, if you think—" Lady Franklin stopped as the male beside Fenella bowed. "Do you know this gentleman?"

"Mother, may I introduce the Earl of Brecken?" Fenella turned to him. "Lord Brecken, this is my mother, Lady Franklin, and my younger sister, Miss Evelina."

The earl bent over Lady Franklin's hand and then took Evie's fingers in his grip. Warmth seeped through her gloves, and her knees weakened. It was like a scene from a romance novel. He leaned over her hand, his burnt umber hair almost black. She could almost feel his breath against her skin.

The well-trimmed beard could not hide the strong jaw and dimple in one cheek. But it was his eyes that held her captive as they glittered dark gold and then green, as the gaslit chandeliers picked up the deep emerald of his waistcoat. She was mesmerized by the flickering shades, recognized the laughter in them, as if she and the earl were new acquaintances who shared an amusing secret.

When he turned to her mother, she felt chilled with the loss of his touch.

"Would you care for some lemonade, ma'am?" His voice was deep and warm, like the welcome heat of the sun on a chilly afternoon.

"That would be divine," gushed Lady Franklin. "Are you new to Town? I'm sure we would have remembered such a fine gentleman."

Fenella and Evelina rolled their eyes in unison.

"I've been traveling for the past few years," he answered politely. "I attended Oxford before that."

"Are you glad to be back in England? I'm sure my daughters would love to hear of your travels. They're well read in the arts."

"I would enjoy that very much," he said, studying Evelina.

She waved her fan to cool her cheeks, positive they matched the color of her gown by now. "What is going on?" she hissed as he stepped away to fetch lemonade for their mother.

Fenella shrugged. "He wanted to meet you. Even promised to dance with me to lessen Mama's anger over..."

She looked away, pressing her lips together to hide a smile. "Anyway, I think he's smitten."

"That's nonsense. We've only just met. And don't you dare laugh." She glared at Fenella.

Lord Brecken returned as the first notes of a waltz sounded over the crowd. Evie's heart leapt as he caught her gaze, apology in his hazel eyes.

"I bribed your sister for this introduction," he murmured just above her ear.

"And what treasure did she think worthy of such a favor?"

"Only a dance. If only most women were so easy to please," he whispered before turning to her sister. "Miss Franklin, would you care to waltz?"

Fenella gave her mother a side look, then shook her head. "I believe Evie would be a much better partner, don't you, Mama?"

"Well, I—"

"It would be my supreme pleasure to dance with Miss Evelina." Lord Brecken held out his elbow expectantly and made a final attempt toward Fenella. "If you're sure?"

Her sister nodded. Evie drew in a shaky breath and laid her fingertips on his arm. A bolt of lightning struck through her core. He stopped to face her once they were surrounded by other couples. Goodness, this man was divine. When he laid his palm against her the small of her back, and claimed her hand in his, she knew a taste of heaven.

"I'm indebted to your sister."

She tipped back her head and raised an eyebrow in question.

"I've been searching for you all evening," he explained.

"Since that first look?" So, he'd felt it too. She shivered at the thought.

Lord Brecken hesitated as if recalling the memory, then nodded and smiled. "Yes, since that first look."

His upturned lips sent her stomach quivering again. "I saw you from across the room with Lord Brooks. Have you known him long?" He pulled her close as they whirled in unison, neatly avoiding another couple. His body, pressed against hers, sent her pulse into a frenzy.

"I knew his younger brother from my time in Belgium several years ago." Another quick turn. "Lord Brooks has been kind enough to accompany me around Town and introduce me to his acquaintances." He chuckled. "Your sister is adept at keeping men at arm's length."

"Oh, no. You saw that atrocious display?" Evie winced. "My sister is—"

"Clever, beautiful, and has a wicked sense of humor. I believe we could be friends."

Evelina peered up at him through her lashes. His tone did not mock; his smile was sincere. She could have kissed the man. "Do you have a brother?" she asked instead with a grin.

"Half-brother several years older, as a matter of fact. My mother was a young widow, and Griffith is from her first marriage." He winked. "Are you matchmaking?"

She shook her head and laughed. "No, I would never assume to understand the workings of another's heart."

"Nor I," he agreed. "My own is enough to contend with."

"Does it speak to you, Lord Brecken?" He intrigued her. His practiced charm, good looks, and honesty were a heady combination.

"Not until recently," he answered and held her gaze, causing her heart to thunder in her ears. "And now, I can't seem to stifle it."

"Oh, my, that is a problem." Evie sensed more to this conversation than light flirtation. She changed the subject, not trusting her reaction to the earl. "Where do you call home, sir?"

"Over the border, near the Brecon Beacons." His eyes

dimmed for a moment. "It's beautiful country, very rural. I didn't think I'd miss it as much as I did."

"You were born in Wales? Your father is Welsh, then?"

He laughed. "No, although he embraced the land and the history more than my mother who *was* born there. He insists that after third or fourth generation, we became Welsh by default."

"How did your family come to be there?"

"My English ancestors backed Henry VII. He rewarded them with lands in Wales, with the promise of continued fealty and protection of the borders. And you?"

Evelina closed her eyes. She was dizzy, either due to the waltz or his warmth against her chest when he held her tight in a fast spin. What a delicious feeling.

The final strains faded, and they stood facing one another, she with a besotted smile on her face and he with a questioning one. Had she missed part of the conversation? He held out his arm again, and she took it, along with several deep breaths. They slowly made their way toward her mother and sister.

"We were discussing family. I told you of my background and it was your turn. I believe that is how conversation works. A back and forth, yes?" Though his expression remained bland, his eyes danced with mirth.

"My mind drifted, enjoying your expertise in the waltz." Evelina wondered if her lack of title would deter his interest. Or was he a fortune hunter that Lady Franklin would approve of? There was nothing for it, so she'd just push ahead. "My father is Sir Horace Franklin. He inherited a baronetcy and works in imports and exports—"

"Franklin and Sons?" Lord Brecken stopped, his mouth open. "The shipping wizard who could procure almost any obscure item for the right price? Even my favorite French brandy."

She laughed. "Yes, that would be my father. Do you know him?"

"Of him. A friend of mine speaks highly of Sir Horace. Insists his wife would have left him during the war if it hadn't been for the goods your father provided." He gave her an appraising look. "Do you have any other siblings?"

She shook her head. "No, he says he's quite satisfied with two daughters."

"Yet, your sister cannot inherit the baronetcy. There must be some disappointment to that end."

Again, she shook her head. Or was he balancing Papa's accounts in his head? "He and my grandfather removed the entail. However, the companies are his main concern, and those will stay with us. I suppose Fenella will end up overseeing the businesses."

"Really? Not her husband?"

Evelina bristled at the disbelief in his tone. "Yes, really. He's raised her as a son, and she's gained some of his *wizardry*, but in numbers."

"She can balance a ledger?"

"She can calculate a column of figures in her head to a farthing *and* faster than any man with a pencil and paper." She smiled smugly at his surprise. "Not all women are muttonheads."

"No, certainly not. My own mother is proof of that. I apologize if I sounded... condescending. It wasn't my intention." His eyes dimmed to light brown before he continued walking. Genuine remorse, perhaps? "So what is your talent?"

"Mediation," exclaimed Fenella as they arrived back at the refreshment table. "Evie keeps us tolerating each other. No one can intervene and soften a disagreement like my sister. It's a gift."

"That's an impressive skill. We could have used you

during the war." He winked, deepening the dimple in his right cheek. "You could have been our secret weapon."

Evelina blushed at his direct regard. She swore he glimpsed her racing heart, heard the panicked thoughts inside her head. He affected her like no other man she'd ever met. Not that there was an extensive list of gentlemen she knew personally, but she'd had her share of admirers. In Bath last summer, there'd been the Scottish shipmaker's boy... but Lord Brecken was a mature man. A strong, handsome, virile man with a sinful smile and the most intoxicating eyes. A sigh slipped from her lips.

"Are you feeling well, Miss Evelina? May I get you a lemonade?" His velvet tone caressed and jangled her nerves, and his fingers at her elbow sent heat roaring up her neck.

Fearing her cheeks were as red as the strawberries she loved so much, Evie only nodded and gave him a grateful smile.

"He is monstrous attractive. And so tall," babbled her mother. "Fenella, you really should accept if he offers to dance the next set."

"That was the last set, Mama," she murmured, but her gray eyes were centered on Evie. "Besides, he'd only be staring over my shoulder, drinking in my lovely sister."

Lord Brecken returned, preventing a response from her or their mother. He stayed a few more minutes, thanked the ladies for their company, then made his excuses.

At the end of the evening, he found them as they waited for the carriage. The chilly air created white clouds of frosted breath while their mother chatted about the on-dits overheard that evening. Lord Brecken approached, his dark greatcoat billowing behind as his long strides ate up the distance between them. *So masculine,* Evie thought with a shiver that had nothing to do with the temperature. Removing his beaver hat, the earl bowed.

"I hope to meet you again, lovely ladies." His hazel eyes were deeper brown in the darkness, and they locked with Evie's. Heat washed over her face, warming her cold cheeks. "Will you be at the Wilkerson's on Friday?"

"We received an invitation to the musical," announced Lady Franklin. "I believe we gave a favorable response."

"Wonderful," he murmured as he took Evelina's hand and kissed her glove again. To his credit, he did the same to her sister and mother. "Until we meet again, then."

He strode away, three pairs of eyes pinned to his back.

Their coach pulled up, and the footman helped the trio inside. Evie leaned back against the gold velvet squabs. Her mother settled next to her, and Fenella settled across from them, trying to fold herself into the corner. Would Mama begin with an onslaught of questions about the earl or admonish her eldest daughter first?

"Don't think you can disappear into the shadows, young lady. How dare you frighten off one of the few men I convinced to ask you to dance. I don't understand you at all." Lady Franklin shook her head, her lashes beginning the familiar martyred flutter. "At least consider your sister. How will she find a good match when you strive to be the pariah of the season? Again!"

"I think it's ridiculous that Evie can't be courted until I marry." She crossed her arms, turning her gaze out the window. "If I were you, Mother, I'd concentrate on your youngest daughter snaring that title for you. She'll make a much better wife for a lord than I would."

"To be clear, I said she couldn't marry before you, but I'm beginning to agree," chided her mother. "I *did* allow her to dance with Lord Brecken tonight after *you* refused."

"I didn't refuse. I just suggested Evie would be a better partner."

"You don't give the gentlemen a chance, Fenella. You are

so afraid of rejection that you push them away before they have a chance to like you." Evelina kept her voice quiet but steady.

Fenella rolled her eyes. "Exactly my point. This is torture for me."

"Well, I'm afraid you have won this time. The on-dits portray you as an eccentric bluestocking. *Eccentric.* I've worked so hard to make a respectable life for us." Lady Franklin moaned and fell back against the cushions, clutching the arm strap. "And what do I get in return? A churlish daughter who debates my every suggestion."

Evelina's heart went out to her sister. It was true Mama hoped to improve her *own* social status, but it had nothing to do with the happiness of her daughters. She dreamed of being one of the *ton*. Although Sir Horace's wealth had opened many doors for his wife, she'd never been satisfied. A baronet was not a peer. Yet, Evie knew her mother loved both her daughters.

"Tell us about Lord Brecken. He seemed quite smitten with you, Evie," Fenella suggested, her eyes smoky and pleading.

"If you think you can change the subject—"

"Did you know Lord Brecken's crest goes back to Henry VII, Mama?" Evelina laid her fingers on her mother's arm, hoping to turn her away from Fenella. "He also has a half-brother."

Peace prevailed as Evelina recounted her conversation with the earl. The knot in her stomach lessened as her sister's shoulders relaxed. It would be a brief respite unless Fenella found a beau. Or Evie gave in and married first. Either scenario would make their mother happy. Yet, the image of a tall, lovely, blonde spinster hovered before her. No, she could not find love before her sister.

Evelina said a quick prayer to find a solution that would satisfy both Fenella and her mother, then snorted. It would be easier to turn water into wine.

CHAPTER SIX

*M*adoc crumpled the paper and scowled fiercely at the roaring fire. He and a close confidante were enjoying a leisurely evening at White's. After a profitable evening of gaming, they'd found a quiet place to talk and enjoy an evening drink. He'd remembered the envelope tucked inside his coat pocket while they waited for the decanter.

"Bad news, Doc?" asked Kit, his dark eyes teasing as he loosened the folds of his cravat with a finger. "It's rare to see such a storm darken your face. I'm accustomed to the jovial yet bland expression you've perfected."

He snorted with good humor at the Earl of Sunderland's observation. "Ha! My invisible armor protects me well. To answer your question, news is rarely good these days."

"Duty or personal?"

Madoc tossed the wadded paper into the flames and watched the edges blacken and curl. "Both. This report from Walters isn't promising. The scoundrels are lying low for now. I'm meeting with him later tonight to find out what he couldn't put on paper. Which reminds me—just between us —what do you know of the Duke of Colvin?"

"The late duke was proper, unbendable, but a good man. His son..." Kit paused as one of the uniformed waiters entered with their port. Once they were alone again, he continued, "His son has lascivious tastes and no conscience, so I've heard. He makes the hairs on the back of my neck prickle when he tries to be friendly. Why do you ask?"

"I met him at Boodle's and had the same impression." Brecken knew he could trust Sunderland, but this was a sensitive case and much of it wasn't common knowledge.

"Boodle's? Hasn't Prinny been seen there lately?"

The Prince Regent was known to prefer London's nightlife to the business of the Crown. His desires and affairs were infamous and the talk of social circles and pubs alike.

"With his entire menagerie," scoffed Madoc.

"Always makes for an interesting evening. I'd steer clear of Colvin, though, if I were you. What of Caerton? Any leads?"

Madoc shook his head. "Walters has a suspicion he's here in London but under a different name. There was a ticket bought under Niall Caerton for passage to Boston. According to the Captain, who happened to be an acquaintance of Walters, a widow and two children occupied the cabin. Left the docks yesterday."

"You think he just wanted his name on the docket to throw you off?"

"It makes sense. Once the ship sets sail, the only proof of passengers is the ledger in the office. The man's not an imbecile. He swindled us out of fifty thousand pounds over the years." Madoc shrugged. "If only the elder Caerton hadn't died."

"So your father took no interest in the estate at all?" Kit

sighed. "What a drastic change from the man I knew. How old was he?"

"Sixty-three." He rubbed the back of his neck. "I should have suspected something when my allowance shrunk each year. But I had blunt from my *extra duties* and enough intrigue to occupy my mind. I assumed Mama would write if anything was amiss."

"Speaking of the countess, how could she not notice the decline of the grounds?"

"The gardens were kept up, and the wing of the castle where she and my father resided." Madoc clenched his jaw. "Clever chancer. She had no idea the stables were being depleted or the livestock sold off. She'd become a recluse along with my father. If Niall had just skimmed the ready, and left the herds and crops alone, I wouldn't be at sixes and sevens."

"In the meantime, may I loan you the cost of a razor?" Sunderland asked with a smirk.

He laughed and rubbed the dark growth on his jaw. "I grew it for an assignment and decided I rather liked it. My valet detests it and hovers over me every morning with a razor and one raised brow. Says I look like a pirate."

"Ha! The ladies might like that," added Sunderland with a grin, his midnight hair gleaming in the flickering light. "The mysterious adventurer."

Madoc gave a half-grunt, half-chuckle. Outside, a light snow blanketed the filth of the city, creating an illusion of innocence. Even St. James Street seemed untouched and pure. "I've been instructed that as an indulged, unmarried heir, I will want to spend much of my time in London. Hence, my gambling tonight. I was in a bloody sweat when I thought I had lost that pile of coin."

"Where did you say you were staying?"

"I've got rooms at the Clarendon for now, but I hope to find something for a little less brass."

"I've heard they have a superb French chef. I might join you for dinner while you're there." Kit's eyes narrowed as he rubbed his jaw. "You know, I might be able to help you out there."

"Eh?"

"I belonged to a private club before I married that provided all the necessities, and then some, for single earls. It's by invitation only. I inherited a membership when my brother died." A flash of pain clouded Kit's dark eyes for a moment. His twin brother, the first Earl of Sunderland, had died after a fall from a horse. He'd left behind not only a grieving brother but a pregnant wife. "Good men, as I recall, but you're out the club once you've been caught in the parson's trap. I believe my friend Lord Darby is still a member. I can introduce you."

"Cheaper than the Clarendon?"

"Rooms are complimentary for members."

Madoc blew out a breath. "That would be beneficial. I cringe every time I place a bet or spend money on something frivolous just to keep up the appearance of wealth."

"I'm happy to help, though my invitation to stay with us still stands."

"I appreciate the offer, but I couldn't impose. I have no idea what kind of company or hours I'll be keeping for the next month or so. I don't want to put your or your lovely wife, Grace, in a bad situation." He threw back the last of the port. "I thank you in advance for the introduction."

"Is it too much for a morning musical?" asked Evelina. The event was at two this afternoon, and it was already past noon. She chewed her bottom lip and studied the ivory walking dress in the Cheval mirror. Two rows of tiny yellow daffodils decorated the hem with a Vandyke collar and cuffs in the same color. A satin ribbon of pale yellow offset the high-waisted gown. "I do wish the neckline was a bit lower. I want to impress without appearing to impress."

Her maid laughed. "Yes, miss." Louella handed her the Devonshire brown hat that matched her pelisse, primping the artificial flowers on the high crown. "You'll be the loveliest girl there."

Evelina accepted the bonnet and matching gloves. "Is Fenella ready?"

"Yes, miss. She's waiting with your mother in the parlor." Louella collected the night clothes and hurried toward the door. "Will a certain gentleman be there?"

Lord Brecken. The earl had interrupted her sleep the past two nights. A waltz that ended with a kiss. A carriage ride that ended with a kiss. A walk in the garden that ended with a kiss. For the love of petunias, the man's wicked grin haunted her as soon as she closed her eyes. After each dream, she'd wake in a sweat, panting. With a smile on her lips.

"He mentioned the possibility, not that it matters." Evie sniffed and tipped her head with dramatic nonchalance. This sent the maid into a fit of giggles.

"You spent an awful lot of time dressing for someone who doesn't matter." Louella balanced the dirty clothes in one hand and reached up with the other to smooth the collar of her mistress's gown. "You'll turn the head of everyone in the room."

"I appreciate the vote of confidence. I wish we could infuse some of that into my sister."

"Miss Franklin will find her way, you'll see." The maid scampered down the hall with a wave.

If only her family was so assured. With a sigh, Evelina

made her way to the parlor. The coach waited outside, and her mother whisked them out the door.

"I need to stop by the milliner's and pick up my new hat," Lady Franklin announced once they were settled, and the driver cracked the whip.

The snow from the night before glittered under the sun's rays, and Evelina squinted at the sparkling lawns as they rolled through Mayfair. The streets were already congested with vehicles and people, and it seemed the whole of London had the same idea to enjoy the lovely afternoon.

Strolling the shopping district was as much about being seen as actual shopping. The luxuries offered along Bond Street were tempting, and its paved walks on each side of the road drew the *ton* in any season. The streets were a muddy mess after a rain or snow melted. Ladies could walk the thoroughfare without fear of filthy hems, enjoy the window displays, and smile at the clusters of young dandies often spread along the length of both Old and New Bond Street.

They stopped in front of a store window with a varied selection of hats, and the driver jumped down to help the ladies from the carriage. Their mother went into the milliner's shop while the sisters strolled arm-in-arm and admired the window displays. They stopped at a jeweler's, *oohing* and *aahing* over a lovely silver necklace with delicate wire twisted into a heart and a cluster of rubies nestled inside. Next to it was a gold pocket watch etched with swirling Celtic designs.

"Papa would like that. What do you think?" Evelina asked, pointing to the watch. She gave Fenella a side glance, but her sister only chewed her lip and fingered the button on her mantle. "Or perhaps he'd like a golden horn to call the elephants to court. I heard it's the latest whim of the Prince Regent."

Her sister nodded, eyes studying the toes of her boots. "Mm-hmm."

"Hallooo." She jabbed Fenella's arm. "What's bothering you?"

Her heart clenched as her sister blinked back tears. "Did Mama say something? Are you worried about seeing Lord Brooks again after your performance at Almack's?"

Fenella shook her head and dragged in a long breath. "I'm going to Scotland."

"What?"

Evie thought back to the past Wednesday. When they'd returned home, both girls had taken the stairs, but Fenella had been called back by their mother. They'd gone into Papa's study. She had assumed her older sister was being reprimanded for her behavior, but never had she thought...

"You're being cast out?" she shrieked.

"Shhh," hissed Fenella. "I'm going to Grandmama's for an extended visit. I'll return after the season."

"Oh, well," she said with a sigh of relief. "Mama is hoping everyone will forget, and you can start with a clean slate next year?"

Fenella nodded. "I didn't say anything before because I didn't know if Papa could arrange it. He'll accompany me next week. I will be home by Christmastide." Her clear gray eyes begged for understanding. "I need this season to be over. I'm tired of... I'm done to a cow's thumb, that's all."

"You must promise to write, or I will be furious." Her mind scrambled to accept this news. Now *she* would be the Franklin on her own during her first season. While Evelina had friends, her closest weren't in the same circles that her mother preferred. Yet, in her heart, she knew she'd be fine. Fenella was shy around strangers, where Evelina never lacked for conversation.

"I promise, but please don't bring it up today. I'm sure

Mother will have plenty to say when she's ready. She may not know Papa told me this morning." She hugged Evie. "I can work in Grandmama's bookstore and escape this circus."

"I'm jealous, you know. I miss her so and love Glasgow. Her pretty neighborhood, the garden behind her house, and the old musty smell of the shop." She glanced over her shoulder to see Lady Franklin emerge from the milliner's, holding the strings of a large hatbox. "It's time to go. Now, smile. You'll soon be safe from musicals, soirees, and all annoying activities that deal with foppish titled men." But as she spoke the words, Lord Brecken's face appeared. Nothing annoying or foppish about that man.

They arrived at the Wilkerson's and waited in line as several other coaches dropped off their occupants. The rowhouse was in the fashionable Mayfair district, and the line of pink or cream homes had a stucco finish. Their destination was pink with a door the color of turquoise and a pineapple frieze above it. A butler stood at the entrance, welcoming the guests.

It was a smaller affair, with a professional musician playing the harp and the youngest daughter, Miss Lavinia Wilkerson, on the pianoforte. Evie didn't care for her and secretly hoped the girl's fingers tripped up on the keys during her performance. The mean-spirited chit had been one of the group to give Fenella so much grief last season.

Once inside, the trio entered the rowhome and handed off their pelisses, muffs, and hats before ascending to the second floor. There were two rooms, one facing the street and the other looking over the back gardens. The guests would mingle and have refreshments in the front room. The recital would be held in the back room.

"He's here," whispered Lady Franklin, tugging on Evelina's sleeve, "and ogling at you."

Evie sucked in a breath and concentrated on smoothing her muslin skirt. "An earl doesn't ogle," she murmured.

After her dreams, she didn't know if she could face Lord Brecken. She peeked through her lashes, and he smiled. That wicked smile. Her heart pounded. How could a man be so striking? He wore a deep gray suit with matching trousers, a ruby and gray striped waistcoat, and a modest cravat. When he moved toward them, her lungs froze. *Breathe!* she thought as snapped open the ivory fan on her wrist. For the love of petunias, she'd never needed her fan so much as this week.

"Good day, ladies," he said with a bow. "May I say you look stunning?"

His eyes glinted brown and gold as they moved from Evie's eyes, down to her toes, and up again. It started a slow burn in her chest and spread up her neck. Her fan fluttered like hummingbird wings over wobbly knees.

"You're quite dashing yourself, Lord Brecken." How did her voice sound so steady and playful? "Are you a music lover?"

"I enjoy the harp but prefer the fiddle. My father had a magnificent baritone that I did not inherit." He winked, his dimple deepening. "When I attempt to sing, it sounds like a wounded bullfrog. It's my secret weapon and only used in dire circumstances."

The women chortled, and Lady Franklin continued the small talk. Evelina observed the darkhaired Welshman as he answered her mother's questions. His profile was like finely carved stone, his nose straight and chin square. Thick dark waves, the color of mocha coffee, were combed straight back and curled at the back of his neck. He had wonderful hands, she observed, large with long slender fingers. They moved gracefully as he spoke, before clasping behind his back.

The doors opened to the second room, and the announcement made.

"I hope you don't mind if I sit with you," he asked Lady Franklin and offered his arm. "I don't have many friends in London who attend these... events. Lord Brooks had other commitments."

"We'd be delighted to have you join us," she said, and her fingers curled over his sleeve.

They made their way down the center aisle, seats flanking them in rows of four. As Lord Brecken stopped at the third row, Lady Franklin reached out, clasped Fenella's wrist, and pulled her toward the chairs. Then she stepped out of the aisle and sat next to her eldest daughter, leaving the earl next to Evelina. Evie closed her eyes at her mother's audacity and wondered whether to pinch her or hug her. The voice in her head screamed in embarrassment; her heart leapt with joy.

She kept her gaze lowered, the white beaded reticule in her lap suddenly of great interest. Her eyes slipped sideways when his hand moved to rest on his lap, his thumb laying on his... fall. She sucked in a breath as he crossed one ankle over a knee, brushing her dress. *Stop staring, you hoyden.* It was too late. She couldn't have dragged her eyes away if someone had shouted, "Fire!" The hem of his trousers hitched up, and he reached down to pull it back over his boot. Evie watched his fingers grip the material, a square gold ring with a **B** studded in tiny diamonds adorning the right fourth finger. The stones seemed to wink at her with his quick movement, and she imagined the pads of his fingers lightly tracing her cheek.

Breathe! she reminded herself for the second time that hour. Gracious, it was stifling in this room. Were there no windows to open? She licked her lips, her mouth as dry as a stone in the Sahara.

"So, are you enjoying your first season, Miss Evelina?"

His voice made her jump, guilt singing her cheeks as she forced her gaze away from his lap and up to his face. She wasn't sure which was a sweeter torture. What would his beard feel like? Would it tickle? His lips would be soft, just like in her dreams. A sigh escaped.

"Is that a yes?" The amusement in his voice snapped her back to reality.

"Heavens, where did my mind wander?" she said, snapping her fan open. Perhaps Papa should invest in ladies' fans. Evie might need several replacements this season.

He bent low, his eyes flashing with challenge, and whispered, "I don't know, but I'd like to come along."

His breath was warm on her cheek and she wondered if he could see the pulse racing in her neck. She wanted to wipe her sweaty palms on her skirt and stopped herself just in time. The surrounding guests hushed, and Mrs. Wilkerson stood in the front of the room. When had everyone taken their seats? When had that lovely elfin girl appeared by the harp?

Mrs. Wilkerson raised her large arms, flapping them in the air, stretching the emerald muslin over her ample hips. "Attention, attention!" Her frizzy brown ringlets jiggled about her plump face as she moved aside to introduce the harpist, a pretty, dark-haired girl with bright blue eyes and an infectious smile.

"For my first song," she began in a thick, German accent, "I'd like to play the Fantasie in C minor, a harp solo written by the celebrated Louis Spohr. I was fortunate enough to study under him when he taught in my hometown of Gotha. I hope you enjoy it."

The first notes of the harp sent a hush over the room. The musician's lids closed, arms raised and poised over the strings. Then her fingers flicked a wire, then another, and the magic began. Haunting strokes rippled through the silence. Her body movement flowed in perfect harmony with the music, almost seductive in the melding of the girl and the melody. Soft and lyrical, then bolder, then harsh, and back to a keening finale. The audience stood and applauded with delighted "bravas!" and "encore, please" as the slight girl rose and curtsied.

At the urging of the crowd, she sat down once again and played another.

"It's rare for composers to write solos for harps," whispered Lord Brecken.

His comment surprised her. "You *are* fond of the harp, then? I thought you preferred the violin."

"My grandmother played and said it spoke the language of love. I used to sit at her feet as a boy and listen." He bent close to her ear, the words hushed as the music continued. His breath washed her skin like a hot summer breeze off the sands of Bath. "Did you know you can feel the vibration of the instrument through the floor? I used to think it was trying to tell me something, but I didn't know the love language. Very disappointing for a young lad."

She pressed her lips together to keep from laughing. "As far as solos, I read the composer's wife is a harpist. He had a vested interest."

Lord Brecken's shoulders shook as he also held in his laughter. "Intelligent man."

When the harpist finished to more resounding applause, Mrs. Wilkerson appeared again. "I now present my daughter, Miss Lavinia Wilkerson, on the pianoforte." Lavinia was a plain girl of medium height, as thin as her mother was round. She had mousy brown hair and thin lips that turned down, giving her the appearance of a perpetual pout.

After her first song, there was a smattering of polite applause. Evelina glanced at Fenella, who sat with her hands clasped on her lap and her jaw taut. Lavinia sat back on the bench, and her mother placed a new stack of music before her. The performance was technically perfect. Yet, she lacked the emotion and appeal of the harpist. By the third selection, the guests were beginning to whisper and fidget.

When she stood and took a final curtsy, thanking her mother and the audience, Lord Brecken mumbled, "All good things must come to an end."

Evelina giggled. "You're a rake, sir."

"So I've been told." He gave her a sly wink.

Heat spread across her chest, and her lips curved in a permanent smile. She wanted to stay in this chair, next to this charming man, and never share him with anyone. At the same time, she wanted to dash out of the room, dump cold water over her head, and hide until the afternoon ended. It would be safer. But Evelina Franklin made decisions according to her heart, not her safety.

As the guests enjoyed refreshments in the front parlor, the hostesses circulated the room. Together, they ambushed the earl. "We were sorry to hear Lord Brooks could not attend, but thrilled you came in his stead. Have you met my daughter, Miss Lavinia Wilkerson?"

Lord Brecken bowed over the girl's gloved hand. Evie noticed with glee that he didn't kiss it.

"I told Mama you should have been in the first row." Miss Wilkerson dipped her head and smiled, revealing protruding teeth. She gave a nod to Evelina and Lady Franklin, but a sneer wiped away the pretense of civility when she glanced at Fenella. "The, er, view would have been much better."

Evie clenched her fists, wanting to slap the silly girl across her cheek.

Lord Brecken grinned and looked down at Evelina. "I'm happy to say I had a splendid view." Then he bowed to both Wilkersons and turned to Fenella. "Would you care to take a stroll? I need to stretch my legs after sitting so long, and you are one of the few people here that can match my stride."

Fenella laughed, then glared at Lavinia. "I'd be happy to. I think that may be the best compliment I've ever received."

"Then there's something wrong with the gentlemen in London." And the two walked away arm in arm.

Evelina's chest swelled at the jealous sparkle in Lavinia's eyes. She was almost disappointed when Lady Franklin came to the rescue and avoided insulting their hostesses.

"Mrs. Wilkerson, where did you find that superb musician? I had to dab my eyes after her performance."

"Thank you, my lady. Dear Mr. Wilkerson discovered her when he was in Germany last year. She's traveling England for the next six months."

"And my dear, when did you become so adept at the pianoforte? I closed my eyes and your divine notes took me to another realm. Such talent for a young girl," gushed Lady Franklin. "You should be very proud of your daughter, ma'am."

"I am, indeed. She's my pride and joy," the woman gushed back, squeezing Lavinia's shoulders.

Catastrophe averted, the Wilkersons continued to mingle, conversing with the other guests. Lady Franklin watched their retreat with narrow eyes. "You should pity the girl rather than goad her, you know. She only wears that smug mask to hide her insecurities."

Evie's mouth fell open at her mother's insight. "Really?"

Lady Franklin nodded. "She looks in the mirror every morning and is terrified no one will ever ask for her hand. It's a fear that you, my dear, will never know or understand."

"And Fenella?"

Her mother snorted. "Once Fenella sees her own beauty, the men will see it too. But at this point, she's her own worst enemy."

"Is that why you're sending her to Scotland?"

Lady Franklin peered down her nose at Evie. "Who told you?"

"Papa told Fenella this morning. She said they leave next week."

"Your grandmother has been lonely since Papa passed. Horace feels Fenella would be company and give her time to—"

"Adjust to your expectations?" It sounded waspish but accurate.

"No, time to realize her potential and where it may lead her. I won't force her into a role she can never be happy with. When Fenella returns, she'll be free to make her choices. I want both my daughters to be happy, despite their insistence to the contrary."

Evie leaned in and kissed her mother's cheek. "I wish you'd say that to Fenella. Or let me tell her it was my insistence she marry first rather than yours."

"She wouldn't listen. Not now." Lady Franklin squeezed Evie's shoulders. "I'm thankful to have one daughter that understands me. I hope someday Fenella and I find the same. But this conversation remains our secret, do you understand?"

Lord Brecken returned with a beaming Fenella on his arm. "Thank you for the intriguing conversation," he said with a slight bow. "Lady Franklin, you and your daughters have been a boon for the day."

"I hope we can be of service again, my lord." With a tip of her head, she notified the footman near the door that they were ready to leave. "Please feel free to leave your card and call on us."

"I plan on it," he said, but his gaze returned to Evie. "I wonder if Miss Evelina and her sister would enjoy a ride in the park? If the weather is fine, I could rent an open carriage."

"I look forward to it," answered Evie. "We could continue our conversation on harps and your grandmother."

Lord Brecken bowed over each lady's hand. When his fingers brushed Evie's, he gave her that spine-tingling smile and kissed her glove. The warmth of his lips sent a jolt up her arm. Heavens! What would her dreams be like tonight?

CHAPTER SEVEN

April 1819

"*A* soiree?"

Madoc ignored Sunderland's amused expression. "Tell me you've never attended one."

"Not willingly." Kit grunted. "There must be a woman involved."

"Of course there's a woman involved. I'm here to find a wife who's flush in the pocket, *and* I can tolerate for the next fifty years," grumbled Madoc.

"And you assume to find this veritable miracle at the Pommerly's soiree?" The Earl of Sunderland lifted the decanter and raised a brow.

"Yes and yes." Madoc held up his glass. "Did I thank you for the brandy you sent? It was a godsend when I was home." He swirled the amber liquid around the cut crystal and inhaled deeply. "Dashed good stuff, Kit."

"My pleasure. Now on to business."

The next two hours were spent going over the ledges of the newly purchased textile mill. The predictions were good, and as long as nothing unforeseen crashed around them, there would be a profit before he ran out of his present funds. It would keep him above water, though the many improvements he had planned would have to wait. At least his tenants would be able to clothe and feed themselves by this time next year, but they would all have to wait for prosperity.

"Shall we join Grace for a drink before dinner?" asked Kit, leaning back against the leather chair to push away from the massive oak desk. "We've invited Darby, so you'll be able to meet him tonight."

"Splendid. Does he have a sister?" He slammed the last book shut and rubbed his eyes with his palms. "One who wouldn't mind leaving the glitter of London for the rural passivity of the Welsh countryside?"

"Yes, to the sister, but I don't think I'd want to deal with Darby. He's quite protective, and the fact you need her dowry wouldn't sit well with him." Sunderland rubbed the back of his neck, as if considering whether to say more. "He's a widower and doesn't trust women. Doesn't trust many men, for that matter."

"Been jilted?"

"In the worst way. She came into the marriage pregnant with another man's child. When he found out the truth, she killed herself." Kit shook his head. "On the wedding night. It was a terrible scandal. Darby embraced the rumors. It kept the *ton* at arm's length."

"Bloody bad luck. It makes my troubles look rosy."

"On to a cheerier subject. I hear you've been frequenting opposing clubs. Sympathizing with Prinny and the liberals at Boodle's and charming the Tories at Whites, or the other way round?"

"I sympathize with myself and getting back to life as it was before the bloody war and my work with the Home Office. Unfortunately, I need to be aware of murmurs on either side of the throne, so I must frequent both clubs. To think the past four years, I've been dreaming of the humdrum, idyllic countryside. Instead, I'm in the smoky dens of London. In truth? I'm tired of looking over my shoulder or wondering what's waiting for me in the shadows." Lifting his glass, the well-practiced smile returned. "Here's to no more spy rings and many long, dull days of leisure in the future. May I never take boredom for granted again."

Sunderland guffawed. "Your days may not be filled with intrigue, but I doubt you'll have much leisure. My estate, properties, and seat in the Lords demand much of my time. You have an even heavier burden, and I don't envy you."

"I've been trained for the title and know what is expected of me. Yet, having the responsibility solely on my shoulders scares the devil out of me." Madoc sighed. "If I failed an assignment, my disappearance would cause little harm. Another man takes my place, and the task is still accomplished. But making decisions that affect the lives of my tenants, people whose livelihood could be crushed by a man's whim..."

The earl nodded. "The obligation can be burdensome at times, but it's our duty to maintain our inheritance, our family name. Those who tend the land and the animals, work within our abodes, are an integral part of the system. Treat them fairly, with the dignity they deserve, and you'll do well. It's that common goal for a better life that will bond you to them."

"Blast, if you don't sound like my father. And a Whig." Madoc laughed. "By the way, how is Grace? Anything I should know before we join her?" He wiggled his eyebrows.

Kit grinned. "She'll tell you herself, but yes, she's with child. I shall have an heir by the end of the summer."

The couple had been married several years, and Grace had miscarried once. It lifted Madoc's spirits to know his friend had a child on the way. "Or a daughter."

"Or a daughter," Sunderland agreed, humor brightening his dark eyes. "As long as she takes after her mother, I won't be disappointed. I'm afraid my face on a female would be a terrible fate."

"True enough," he agreed with a snort. "You still seem happy with the leg shackles. How long has it been?"

"Three years. She's my life's blood, I tell you. Flows through my veins. If you want some words of wisdom, the right woman completes a man. If you can find one you love, you'll be a better man for it." The earl finished off his brandy and set the empty glass on the polished side table with a *thud*.

The Earl of Darby was not what Madoc had expected. A golden-haired, jovial man under thirty years. No self-pity or brooding silences. Yet, there was something in his blue eyes that warned Madoc not to trust the easy smile and polished charm. A hard glint that would make a wise man wary.

Grace, the Countess of Sunderland, entered the room in her usual brisk manner. The sheer silver overlay fluttered over the lilac silk gown. Auburn curls framed her face, and her green eyes landed on Madoc with a smile. She opened her arms wide, sweeping aside formal greetings, and kissed both his cheeks.

"How are you, Doc? Is your mother faring well?" Her genuine concern was one of the traits that made this woman so likeable. She was beautiful, caring, engaging, and yet had the maternal instincts of one much older.

"You are stunning as always," Madoc said as he accepted her embrace. "And my mother is doing better than I expected."

"It's devastating enough to lose your father, but the other catastrophe as well…" She stepped back to inspect him, then leaned back up and whispered, "I'm so glad you've joined Kit in his investment ventures. You'll be swimming in lard in no time."

He laughed. "I hope so, my lady, I hope so. How is Sammy?"

The countess had a younger brother, a bright, precocious boy as Madoc remembered. Grace had raised him since infancy, after their mother died in childbirth.

"Can you believe he's eight already?"

"Going on eighteen," added Sunderland. "This month, the boy insists on boxing lessons. His father's strength is fencing and riding. He wants Sammy to learn from someone with more expertise rather than his home-brewed style."

"You're quite skilled in the ring," Madoc pointed out.

"So Grace informed them. The lad's as tall as Grace already. He'll be a strapping young man in another few years. Instructing him will keep me fit."

"I didn't realize," said Lord Darby. "I frequent Gentleman Jackson's. Shall we set up a match some time?"

Grace giggled. "Those days are over, I'm afraid. I prefer him in one piece."

Sunderland shot her mocking glare. "I still practice at Offley's when I'm in Town. They have an excellent beefsteak and good ale after I've worked up an appetite."

"Good to know," said Darby with a nod. "My lady, how goes the renovation of Sunderland Castle?"

"Almost complete. We began work on the oldest part of the castle last summer. It's been quite… enlightening."

"Trying to ferret out a ghost that she thinks lives in the

original stronghold. The last time I ventured to that area, the hairs on my neck rose. Grace seems to think it's an ancestor." Sunderland laughed, his dark eyes crinkling. "Good God, I hope I don't have that effect on people. But if the days get too tedious for either of you, come to Sunderland Castle. We'll give you the whole north wing."

"No, thank you. I prefer an adversary I can see." Madoc laughed. "Perhaps Lord Darby is more adventurous?"

"My past is haunting enough. I think I'll wait until Lady Sunderland has sent the spirits on their way." His smile didn't reach his blue eyes, but he held up his glass of claret. "To a splendid evening with two of my favorite people and a new friend."

"Here, here!" cried Grace. "Speaking of new friends, will you sponsor Lord Brecken? My husband says the Wicked Earls' Club may be open to new members."

Darby opened his mouth but she continued, undaunted.

"I'm sworn to secrecy, but I wouldn't rest until he told me what *this* stood for." She tapped a gold **W** on her husband's lapel. "He wears it whenever we're in London." She glanced at Kit. "I'm happy to know that the wearer is always someone I could turn to for help, but even happier he is no longer an active member."

"Lord Darby has offered to take me to the club tonight. He's introducing me to the members." Madoc held up his glass and nodded at the blond earl.

"It's been arranged on Sunderland's references and a mutual friend," Darby confirmed. "Several of the men knew of the former Lord Brecken, and one remembers the present Brecken from Waterloo. A set of rooms has just been made available due to a recent marriage."

The butler appeared in the doorway. "Dinner is served, my lord."

✳

The downstairs of the club resembled any other gentlemen's club. There were rooms for gaming, a library for those who preferred a quiet space, and a dining room that served food at any hour. They entered a crowded area with several men engaged in conversation near a fireplace, drinks in hand. Several tables flanked the right side of the room where various games of whist, faro, and hazard were in progress.

"I'll warn you the stakes are often high," Darby said as he nodded at several of the men. "I don't gamble, myself."

"I appreciate the warning." This inconspicuous building, in an inconspicuous neighborhood, with a single **W** above the entrance, would be Madoc's refuge. He could come and go without raising any suspicion.

The meeting with the other members had gone well. He'd had the requisite qualifications—trusted among his peers and claimed the title of earl and bachelor. The benefits included an exclusive floor of this club, a set of private rooms for each, and almost any vice for the asking. He'd recognized one of the men from his days in Oxford. Another had been an acquaintance of his father's. A third... while they had not acknowledged each other, he had worked with the man after the war. His amusement at the name "Wicked Earls' Club" had dissipated. These were not frivolous dandies. Madoc rubbed the shiny new pin on his lapel. It was good to know he could count on these men if needed.

"Now you know the lay of the place. Care for a game of billiards?" asked Darby.

Madoc perked up. "It's been some time since I've played, but that and a ball of fire would be a perfect end to my evening."

"I think that can be arranged. We'll play in the billiards room upstairs, so there are fewer interruptions." Darby took the lead down a hall, then Doc followed him up an enclosed staircase.

Their steps were muffled by the plush wool carpet and thick paneled walls. Coming up to another long hall, there were several doors on either side. These were the private quarters for the earls. The billiards room was rectangular and well-appointed with the table at the far end. Its golden-scrolled legs gleamed in the firelight, ending in lion heads under each of the corner pockets. In front of him, chairs were arranged facing the table in a semi-circle, with a side table and two decanters. By the colors of the liquid, he guessed one to be port and the other brandy. Gleaming linenfold paneling of French walnut surrounded all four sides with Axminster carpet underfoot.

Madoc stroked his finger along the fine green cloth before pulling the three colored balls and the target from the pockets. He picked up one of the two white cue balls and tossed the ivory orb a couple times. "Nice set."

"One of the best in London. Choose your cue," said Darby, "while I pour us a drink."

Madoc found his new friend to be proficient at the billiards. With two wins each, they were on the final game. He poured the last of the brandy into his glass and watched Darby bend, aim, and make a perfect shot. "I'm rather glad you don't like to wager. I think I'm about to lose."

Darby grinned. "I'm having a good night."

"At Sunderland's, you mentioned we had a mutual friend. I had the feeling you didn't mean the earls from the club." Madoc took a chair by the fireplace as the game ended. The flames crackled and danced, and he stretched out his legs, leaning his heels on the hearthstone.

"Walters also works for me." Darby sat down in the opposite chair and relaxed in the same manner. "He highly recommended you as a gentleman of your word and a trustworthy Englishman."

"He's a good man." Doc rubbed his jaw. "How did my name happen into a conversation?"

Darby gave a sheepish grin. "I had to be certain you were a bang-up cove before I sponsored you. I trust Sunderland, but a man can't be too careful these days. I asked Walters to see what he could find out. He confided he was also your man and vouched for you. It was enough for me."

"I'm glad to hear it. This situation is a godsend for my circumstances. I hope to repay you someday."

"We look out for each other," Darby replied, tapping the **W** on his jacket. "Stay true to that code. It's all that's required."

"You must swear to write me every week." Evelina hugged her sister after their mother had completed an endless list of instructions. "I shall miss you so."

Fenella smiled. "You will be too busy with suitors to think about me. This has worked out for the best, you'll see." She climbed into the carriage and waited for her father. Their trunks were tied on top of the conveyance, letters safely packed to her grandmother and other relatives, and some fresh biscuits from Cook wrapped in paper.

Fenella blinked, a watery smile on her face. "I love you, little sister. And thank you. For everything."

Sir Horace bustled down the steps, tall and elegant as usual, as he placed a hat on his silver-streaked blond hair. "Finish up those goodbyes, you mawkish females," he teased as he embraced first his daughter and then his wife, giving the latter an enthusiastic farewell kiss.

He climbed in and settled across from Fenella. Tapping

the roof with his cane, the carriage lurched forward and another round of waves began until the vehicle disappeared around a corner. Both women stood silently for a few minutes, lost in their own thoughts. A piece of Evie's heart had just left for Scotland.

Lady Franklin pulled her shawl tight and turned toward the veranda steps. "I'll miss that man," she mumbled as she entered the hall.

Evelina grinned. "We have invitations," she said stopping at the side table and poking through the envelopes and calling cards on the silver tray. Her finger flipped one over and her breath caught. She picked up the small card with the simple engraving:

Earl of Brecken

One corner of the card was folded over. He had delivered this himself. When? "Mama!"

"Oh, my dear! He must have left it early this morning. I bet he went on an early morning ride and dropped it off." She clapped her hands to her face. "He'll call on us this afternoon, I imagine."

Evelina's heart quickened at the thought. "I need to change. I can't greet him like this." She picked up her skirt and ran up the stairs, a surprisingly agile Lady Franklin right behind her. "Louella, Louella, come quickly."

"I believe Lord Brecken is smitten."

"Don't be ridiculous, Mama. There are dozens of lovely ladies out this season. I am only one of many." Even as Evelina said the words, she hoped they weren't true. Was he only pitching her the gammon? "Why would he consider me? He could have the daughter of an earl or possibly even a marquess."

"I don't believe he needs the dowry. His clothes and

accessories are of the finest quality. He doesn't own a house in the city, but many rent for the season. I had your father inquire into the family, and there's no rumor of gambling. It's an old, respected name." She laid her hand on Evie's cheek. "Perhaps he's drawn to your beauty and wit?"

Evelina snorted. She was certainly drawn to his. "I still believe I should wait until Fenella is married before I *think* about courting *any* gentleman."

"Said the girl who ran up those stairs faster than a fox in a hunt." Her mother chuckled. "I can't blame you. He's a fine-looking man."

"With a fine title," Evelina muttered under breath. It wasn't as if she was setting her cap for him. She only wanted to improve her skills in flirtation. Yes, that was it. If he was only cutting a wheedle, then she would use him in a like manner.

Evie thought of the dreams that continued to fill her nights. If he ever *did* kiss her in the flesh, would it be as good as in her fantasies? For the love of petunias, how would she hide her disappointment?

CHAPTER EIGHT

"The Earl of Brecken," announced the butler.

Evelina drew in a sharp breath, then stood to shake out any wrinkles in her pale rose skirt. Two rows of tiny white buds, sewn in vertical stripes down the front of the dress, curved out in opposite directions to create the illusion of a split skirt. White lace adorned the modest neckline and sleeves. She toyed with the cameo on her chest as he appeared in the doorway. His indigo jacket and fawn pantaloons hugged his muscular frame; shining black boots and a matching hat gave him a jaunty air.

"Heavens," muttered Lady Franklin, "what a specimen."

Evie smiled gratefully at her mother and stifled a giggle. It was just what she needed to shake off her nerves. "My lord, how good of you to call."

He moved forward and bowed. "Miss Evelina, Lady Franklin, I trust I'm not interrupting?"

"Of course not, this is our day at home. Please, sit. It's been a dreary day, so tell us something entertaining to take our mind off the morning." Her mother sat back down,

87

folded her hands in her lap, and looked expectantly at the earl.

"I'm afraid I haven't much to report." He paused, rubbing his beard, then held his pointer finger in the air. "Ah! Did you hear Lord Thurstin's youngest son challenged the Duke of Neville's son to a race? They met early this morning at Rotten Row and chased the grooms off who were exercising their masters' horses. They took off just as the authorities ran to stop them. I was told there were at least two dozen spectators there to watch, all placing bets."

Evelina covered her mouth. Horses and carriages were always to maintain a sedate pace in Hyde Park. The grooms of aristocracy were allowed to exercise horses early in the morning, but for safety reasons, the rule was in place for the rest of the day. "Oh my, Lord Thurstin will be irate. His youngest is known for daring exploits."

Lady Franklin laughed. "Oh, how I love a good race. There's nothing wrong with young Corinthians feeling their oats occasionally."

"Any on-dits in return?" asked the earl, his eyes on Evelina.

"Nothing nearly so exciting. My sister and father left for Scotland this morning. She'll be staying with my grand-mother for a long visit." She paused, casting a side glance at her mother at her mention of a relative in Scotland.

"Nothing serious with your grandmother's health, I hope?"

"Only loneliness," she assured him.

"I'm certain Miss Franklin will chase the blue devils away."

A knock at the door and the butler announced, "Mrs. Wilkerson and Miss Wilkerson."

Evie fought to keep her disappointment hidden, knowing

the earl would follow protocol and not linger once the new guests were ushered in.

Lady Franklin rose, an apology in her smile. "Oh, please show them in."

As the Wilkersons entered, Lord Brecken stood and bowed. "Ladies, it's a pleasure to see you again."

Mother and daughter both smiled, questions in their eyes at the earl's presence. "We're surprised we haven't seen you in Hyde Park, my lord. Lavinia enjoys afternoon rides now that the weather is improving."

"He prefers to ride early in the morning." Lady Franklin spoke for the earl as if they were old friends.

"I'll walk you out," intervened Evelina, hoping the earl hadn't taken offense.

As the butler held the door open, Lord Brecken paused on the step. "I wondered if you would accompany me next Tuesday afternoon? Mrs. Wilkerson is quite right about Hyde Park. The weather is much improved, and I could bring round an open carriage." Another pause. "Lady Franklin is welcome, of course."

Pish and petunias, I hope not, Evie thought. "I don't believe I have any other obligations. I accept your kind offer."

He bowed over her hand again and trotted down the steps. "Until then," he called with a final wave.

In the parlor, the conversation was lively. Mrs. Wilkerson had the same aspirations as Lady Franklin, so they were two rival peas in a pod when they were together. "Lord Brooks has shown a decided interest in Lavinia. Why, she could be a baroness by Michaelmas."

"Mama, don't put the cart before the horse. It's only been a ride in the park and several dances," Lavinia scolded before turning to Evelina. "It seems Lord Brecken has established an interest?"

"Another cart before the horse," said Evie, though the

satisfaction in Lavinia's eyes irritated her. "He did ask me to drive with him on Tuesday, however. If Mama approves?"

"Of course, my dear. Nothing would please me more." Lady Franklin gave Mrs. Wilkerson a smug smile. The competition between them was almost comical. "To think, my friend, your daughter a baroness and mine a *countess*. How divine."

Lavinia's lips pressed together, but she gave Evelina a contrite glance. "I came along today to apologize, only to find Fenella's gone. I don't know what got in to me at the musical." She let out a martyr-worthy sigh. "I suppose I'll have to wait... unless *you* could mention it in a letter when you write?"

"I'd be happy to include a personal note from you, of course." What a sham! If Lord Brecken *was* interested in Evie, he may resent any callousness toward her sister. Miss Wilkerson hadn't been kind that afternoon. Lord Brooks and Lord Brecken were chums. Lavinia had her sights on the baron and didn't want to appear peevish in his eyes. The chit didn't fool anyone.

Evelina smiled sweetly as Lavinia opened her mouth, then shut it, wisely choosing not to pursue the subject. If only Evie could be a fly on the wall when Fenella received that note from Miss Wilkerson.

The carriage dress of primrose yellow highlighted her dark honey-brown curls to perfection. Evelina adjusted the straw bonnet so it tilted just so... "Where's the parasol? The sun is out today, and we'll be in an open carriage."

"Calm yourself, miss. It's not as if he's the first gentleman to take you for a ride," said Louella as she fetched the parasol and reticule for her mistress.

Only the first to imperil my heart, she thought as she pushed her hand through the clutch of her reticule. Mama had declined the invitation, which made Evie anxious—in a good way. Sort of.

"Though I don't blame you none, he's very fine indeed," added the maid. She held the wrist loop of the reticule open while her mistress slid her wrist through it.

"He's here," called her mother up the stairs. "Hurry, now. Don't make him wait."

She rolled her eyes at her mother's impatience, but hurried down the hall when the butler's deep voice announced the earl. Evie descended the stairs, and all thought vanished. Her world narrowed to those golden-brown eyes that flashed green and the breathtaking smile. Her heart pounded, and the wings in her belly took flight again.

"Miss Evelina, you are sunshine on a dark day," he murmured as he bowed over her hand. "Are you sure you won't join us, Lady Franklin?"

"No, but I thank you for the offer. Enjoy this lovely afternoon."

And it was a beautiful day. They arrived to a dozen carriages and riders crowded along Rotten Row, making it difficult to stop and talk with acquaintances. Others strolled near the Serpentine.

"How are you adapting to life without your sister?" asked Lord Brecken.

"I shall endure, though I'm jealous. I haven't seen my grandmother since last summer. I doubt if I'll be able to visit this year." She giggled. "Fenella will come back with Grandmama's thick Scottish brogue and drive poor Mama mad."

"This is your maternal grandmother?"

She nodded.

"Lady Franklin is a Scot? I'd have never guessed. She sounds so..."

"English? She's half and half. My grandfather came from Manchester." Evelina rolled her eyes. "My mother hates Scotland and her merchant beginnings—my grandparents have owned a bookstore in Glasgow for forty years. Mama considers all Scots as coarse brutes and strives to be very English. She even hired a tutor when she married Papa to teach her how to speak and behave like the aristocracy."

"The Scots have much in common with the Welsh. Both are strong, stubborn, and like a good fight. My father was English by blood but raised as Welshman. He rarely took his seat in the House of Lords, preferring the wilds of Wales."

"Do you have any siblings?"

"I never had any sisters, and my half-brother, Earl of Griffith, didn't live with us."

"But why?" She couldn't imagine being alone as a child. Fenella was her best friend and confidante.

"Griff's grandmother insisted he should live in his ancestral home and be raised on his own lands. When my mother remarried, there was a terrible argument, and it seems the dowager countess won. They have not spoken since, preferring correspondence when necessary to any actual conversation."

"That's horrible." How could one mother be so vindictive to another?

He shrugged. "Griff spent the summers with us and seemed to accept the situation. He said in medieval times boys didn't live with their mothers and were sent away at the age of eight to train as a page. He defended his grandmother, insisted that she was fulfilling his father's wishes. Griff wasn't yet two when my mother became the Countess of Brecken, and Lady Griffith doted on him."

"It must have been hard for your mother."

"I don't know, to tell you the truth. As a child, I remember her being very pretty and happy. She smiled and laughed often until my father's accident." A shadow passed over Lord Brecken's face.

"What happened?" she asked, putting a hand on his arm. "If you don't mind talking about it?"

He told her of the accident, his father giving up, his mother's sole focus on bringing him back. His voice turned husky as he spoke of the late earl giving up on life because his legs had failed him. He kept his eyes on the path as he spoke, and she was glad not to see the anguish that would surely be there.

"But the man you knew and loved did return in the end?" It wasn't exactly a silver lining, but it was better than the late earl dying without resolution with his loved ones.

He nodded. "Yes. Yes, he did." He switched the reins to one hand, slowed the horses, and covered her glove with his own. "Thank you for listening. I haven't spoken of his passing much, not the circumstances, anyway."

Evie gazed into his hazel eyes and glimpsed the vulnerable boy he had been once. She wanted to cradle his face in her palms and tell him all would be well. They regarded each other, a moment in time suspended. Oh, how she wanted him to kiss her. Press his lips to hers.

His hand lifted, his knuckles tracing the outline of her jaw. "So soft," he murmured. "Do you have some kind of magical powers that draws me to you?"

His touch stole her breath, so she shook her head.

"I don't believe you," he said, his voice husky, his eyes a smoky amber.

His breath fluttered against her cheek. Her fingers reached up of their own accord and stroked the soft beard along his chin. She moved up, one pad tracing his bottom lip, cursing the gloves that blocked her touch. He sucked in a breath as if in pain and she jerked her hand back. He caught it in his. "I'm sorry. You're bewitching me, Miss Evelina." His eyes were glued to her mouth; his head bent—

"Hullo, there, Brecken," called a male voice.

Evie jumped, aware of her surroundings again and not just the man beside her. Coming toward them was Lord Brooks and Miss Wilkerson. Brooks looked over his shoulder, saw no one behind them, and pulled his conveyance to a halt.

"It seems most of London had the same idea today. It was like getting down Oxford Street earlier. I'm glad the traffic has thinned." Lord Brooks and Lavinia smiled at the same time, and Evelina bit the inside of her lip to keep her mouth closed. She hadn't noticed how similar they were in appearance. Pish and petunias, they were a match.

"You remember Miss Evelina?" asked Lord Brecken of Brooks before turning to the lady. "I hope he's being the perfect gentleman, Miss Wilkerson?"

"Oh yes," she said with a bob of her head, brown curls bouncing off her cheeks beneath the wide-brimmed bonnet. "Lord Brooks is a skilled driver and has such entertaining stories."

"Will I see you at Boodle's later this week?" asked Brooks.

"Without a doubt," said the earl. The couples bade farewell and parted ways.

"Do you think he's interested in Miss Wilkerson?" he asked as they trotted off.

"According to Mrs. Wilkerson, he's very interested." *In her dowry*, she thought. "So men don't talk about these things with each other? I mean, like women do? Fenella has always insisted that men gossip as badly as women."

Lord Brecken let out a loud guffaw. "We don't always confide our *own* secrets. But the clubs are full of rumors and the latest scandals. The only thing men prefer to the latest on-dits or sports is a good wager."

"You mean at the tables? Or horse races?" she asked, enjoying the conversation as much as his handsome profile.

"I'll tell you a secret." He glanced over his shoulder, then to either side, as if making sure no one was listening. "Last week, at a club that shall remain anonymous, a certain viscount finished his meal and proceeded to the faro table. He had a dob of gravy on the end of his nose."

"Oh, my," she giggled. "That is truly scandalous."

"But wait, there's more. Another baron, who will also remain anonymous, bet his friend how long it would take for the viscount to discover the gravy and wipe it off." Lord Brecken bent his head close to her ear. "The bet was for 100 sovereigns."

Her mouth fell open. "For gravy on someone's nose?"

He nodded. "Within the hour, there was over a thousand gold coins hovering on the tip of the viscount's nose."

"What happened?"

"A newcomer entered the room—"

"Who will also anonymous," added with Evie with glee.

Lord Brecken laughed. "Exactly. He didn't know about the wager and told the viscount about the remains of dinner on his nose." He laughed and shook his head. "No one had bet whether someone would tell him, so all bets were off."

"I'll have to write Fenella and tell her she was right. Males can be just as mutton-headed as females."

Mid-April 1819

"How is Miss Wilkerson?" Madoc and Brooks were enjoying

a dinner at White's. "I didn't think you were perusing the market."

Brooks nodded, a brown curl falling across his forehead. He pushed it back and took a long draw from his ale. "On the contrary, I'm in the same predicament as you, dear friend. My father was rather fond of the tables and possessed no luck or skill. While your situation is not common knowledge, mine is. I thought you knew."

He shook his head. "When it comes to the London circles, I only know what you tell me or I've gleaned from other conversations."

Doc's brows furrowed. It made sense. "That's why you offered to dance with Miss Franklin."

Brooks gave a mock shudder. "Yes, her dowry is quite a bit larger than Miss Wilkerson's, though she'd make sure any man earned it. She won't be easy. Instead, I'll take a little less blunt and a more malleable wife." He tipped his head and tapped his lips with his napkin. "You've set your cap for Miss Evelina, haven't you? Sir Horace made it known the eldest daughter was to marry first, which was why the dowry was so large."

"Miss Franklin's off to Scotland for an undetermined amount of time, and I'm not close to making an offer on the younger."

"Does the dowry, er, transfer to Miss Evelina?"

"I assumed..." *Blast!* He didn't know.

"The Franklins may assume their youngest's beauty will save them blunt. She could do well with a liberal, yet not princely sum."

"I rather need the princely sum." He blew out a loud breath. "Better to find out sooner than later."

"It seems I have a mission, then. Is my face clean?" asked Brooks with a smirk.

"It is," Brecken told him with a chuckle. "Though an

unscrupulous man might not tell you if it wasn't. You could save me from the leg shackles altogether with a well-placed piece of egg on your cravat and a room full of bored, well-breeched aristocrats."

"Lawks! It may be a scheme worth considering if both our dowries fall through. In the meantime, I'll put in some discreet inquiries and find out what plans Sir Horace has for his youngest daughter."

"I appreciate it."

Brooks paused. "Let me give you fair warning. One's finances aren't kept in the dark for long. Your secret will be found out sooner than later. Do you know when Sir Horace returns?"

"No." If Miss Evelina didn't have the brass, he'd have to continue his search. The idea made his chest ache. Though he had been careful not to come close to another kiss, she invaded his thoughts throughout every day. A flash of sandy-brown hair, a glimpse of topaz orbs made his pulse quicken until he realized it wasn't her. The image of her full lips turned up in a smile, her ivory skin, those full curves stoked his desire at night, and he woke aching with need. There was no doubt she held him in her affection. He knew women well enough to recognize the passion in her eyes. Would it make a difference when she discovered he was cleaned out? Worse, would she doubt his growing affection?

The *what-ifs* could drive him mad. He could be honest with her. Brecken snorted to himself. Or wait until he was certain of her regard, *then* tell her the truth.

How could he give her up?

How could he *not* keep a deathbed promise to his father?

CHAPTER NINE

May 1819

*M*adoc entered The Guinea, found a back table, and winked at the barmaid. Along one wall, a cheery fire blazed in an enormous hearth. Two large iron pots hung at each end, the smell of bubbling stew mingled with sweat and stale ale. Patrons clustered around the fireplace, a loud shout or guffaw rising above the steady din. There were employees from the mills and shops, street cleaners, delivery men, all workers necessary to the city for their menial labor.

The pub was also a favorite haunt for the staff of the wealthy. Grooms and footmen could complain about their masters without fear and share secrets about the titled families who paid their wages. Located on the outskirts of Mayfair, it was just far enough that their employers would never wander in. Close enough, and costly enough, not to attract thugs from the Rookeries.

"Some days you're harder to recognize, my lord," Walters said as he plunked a bumper of ale onto the table. "If I didn't know better, I'd think ye like playing dress up."

Madoc snorted. "I got used to the scratchy wool long ago. It's the rented hackneys that can be torture. Never know what you'll find—or smell—in one of those cabs."

Tonight, he was a factory worker in a cotton shirt, brown homespun trousers, and a threadbare wool coat and cap. He'd stopped in the alley and scraped his fingers on the ground to dirty his nails, brushed off the excess on his back-side, and pulled on fingerless gloves.

"It'll be a shame when ye give it up. I swear ye have common blood somewhere in your ancestry." The investiga-tor's dark eyes twinkled at the jest. Before the war, Walters had been a Bow Street runner until he found too much evidence on a crime involving a nobleman. A false charge of accepting bribes had quickly followed Walters' report. Now he worked for the private sector—and ironically, the Home Office—but still held a grudge against certain members of the higher class.

"We've had some adventures, my lord. I'll miss working with ye." He pulled a hat off his unruly brown hair, the wall sconce highlighting the early streaks of silver at his temples. "I have good news, I think."

"Personal?"

"Aye, and the other." Walters grinned at the barmaid as she passed by and dropped another cup of ale next to his elbow. Her fingers trailed up his sleeve in a familiar fashion as she walked away. He was well-known in this tavern; much of his information, directly or indirectly, came from the patrons. As one of them, he could coax them into discourse much easier than a constable or even a man with deep pock-ets. A matter of trust, Walters had explained.

"The pair I've been following and their friend, the duke,

seem to be in the devil's palm together. I believe His Grace is providing funds for the radicals." He ran a hand through his thick curls. "If ye'd be so kind as to accompany me, I'll show you what I've learned. Then you can write your report. With the implication of the Duke of Colvin, this will fall under another's jurisdiction. Someone with more authority than you, my lord. You'll be out of it in short time."

"It can't be soon enough. This is good news." Relief washed over him, but he still worried for Walters. The man took chances, and he hoped the Crown's next representative appreciated the ex-Bow Street Runner. "What about you?"

"If my guess is correct, I know who'll take your place. I've served under him before. He's a good man." Walters checked his pocket watch. "The performance should be finished soon. The duke usually leaves the theater and has his carriage wait for him in the piazza at Covent Garden. He never goes to the same brothel two nights in a row, so we'll need to be there to follow him."

"Are we on foot?"

"Aye, if ye don't mind. It's less conspicuous." Walters threw a coin on the table and stood, placing his cap on his head and pulling it low. Madoc did the same.

They left the Guinea and strode quickly toward the market. The well-tended shops and homes faded into tenements and older buildings where shopkeepers had their business on the ground floor and their living quarters above. Only a few streets led to the square. These were narrow and dark, lit only by the weak light shining through covered or draped windows. Here were the gaming hells that sent wealthy men fleeing the country over enormous debts and houses where an abbess catered to any sexual desire or whim for a price.

In the morning, these alleys would be crowded with costermongers hauling their wares and customers vying for the best produce and cheapest prices. Closer to the piazza would be the coffeehouses and bawdy entertainment the *ton* frequented for titillating adventure. There was sometimes less than a block that separated most of the visiting *beau monde* from the seedy part of the district.

Tonight, men in search of drink, gaming, and women lurked in the shadows. Doxies leaned in doorways, calling out to passersby. Madoc peered up at the moonless sky. The fog was heavy tonight, making visibility poor. A perfect night for thieves and pickpockets. They reached the piazza and found a shadowed corner to wait. It didn't take long.

A coach appeared with a gold enameled **C** on the black lacquered door. A tall, dark-haired man stepped out, his black silk hat set low, his collar pulled up.

"That's him," whispered Walters. "If he meets up with his Spencean friends, it's always after the theater at a coffee-house. He takes information from them and then moves on to a brothel."

They waited for Colvin to pass, his long coat flowing behind him, cutting a path in the gray mist. He stopped in front of a shop and peered inside, before opening the door and entering. Walters and Madoc waited a few minutes, then followed. Voices competed to be heard over the din, and they squinted against the smoky atmosphere. Many of the customers here were a step up from the Guinea. They wore waistcoats and cravats, and while they still worked for a living, it wasn't manual labor. Walters settled at the end of the wooden counter, blending in with the rest of the patrons. Madoc slid in next to him and ordered a pint for each of them.

He sipped the dark porter and watched the duke over the rim of his cup. Two other men sat at the small table with him, all three heads bent together. Madoc recognized the dark hair and hawk nose of one man, Arthur Thistlewood, a prominent member of the Spencean Philanthropists. He'd already been involved in suspicious activity so it was no surprise. Thistlewood shook his head vigorously, and the duke stood. The second man stood also and said something that made the duke sit down again. An envelope was passed across the table and Colvin slid it inside his greatcoat. Fifteen minutes later, all three men left the coffeehouse. Madoc and Walters tossed back the rest of their porter and did the same.

"There," said Walters. He pointed to a dark alley where the duke disappeared. "Now, he'll pass that letter on to someone else."

"How often does this happen?" asked Madoc.

"About once a month." Walters patted his side. "Ye brought your weapon, my lord?"

"Do you need to ask?"

They crossed the street and followed Colvin. He stopped at the entrance of dead-end alley. A young boy stepped from the shadows, they spoke, and the duke reached inside his coat and handed the lad the envelope. The boy tipped his cap and ran off. Colvin continued down the dank alley and knocked on a side door. When someone answered, he entered. Madoc and Walters leaned against a building across from the brothel.

Fog looped around their boots, and a slimy moisture soaked into the back of their coats. It brought back memories of past missions. He was glad this part of his life was coming to an end.

"Do you want to wait and see what he does after this?" asked Walters.

"No, I can write my report. I have no interest in the lascivious activities of the duke." Madoc looked around the dead-end. "Let's get out of here. I've got a bad—"

Click! Two men emerged from behind stacked oak barrels, blocking their exit. The glint of metal told Madoc at least one had a pistol. He was glad he'd slipped the knife into his boot.

"G' ev'ning, ge'lmen," said the tallest. His crooked nose and missing tooth spoke of past scuffles and near-misses. "What brings ye to our li'l establishment?"

"We thought we were up for a bit o' excitement," said Walters. "But I fear it's too rich for me blood. Me wife's none to pleasant if I spend the whole week's wage."

"Aye, I have a missus that always wants wot I can't give 'er," chimed in the second thug, gripping a thick wooden club.

"We'll just be goin' then," said Walters with a tip of his cap.

"No' quite yet," said the big man, tapping the barrel of his gun against his leg. "Our employer don't like folks followin' him. Our job is t'make sure 'e knows who has an interest in 'im." He stepped forward with the pistol cocked. "So, we'd like ye t'take a friendly li'l walk wi' us."

The two others appeared behind the casks. A tall, lanky man swinging an iron bar and a short, stocky man brandishing a blade in each hand. Madoc bent his knees and withdrew his dagger. *Shhht!* If he tried for his pistol, the big brute would get a shot off at one of them. He hunched his shoulders and shook out his arms as the four men circled. He and Walters put their backs to one another, each facing two of the attackers.

"It's only two to one. We'll spill a bit of claret and be on our way," said Madoc. His muscles tensed, then relaxed as his body prepared for the fight to come.

"Aye, I've been craving a good mill, but these smelly ruffians will do." Walters was tossing his blade from hand to hand. He always preferred to wait and react.

Madoc was the opposite and preferred to be the aggressor. He thrust out his arm and grabbed the wooden club, pulling the smaller man off balance. Madoc turned on his heel, pushing the club and the man into the large thug with the gun. A shot rang out. Behind him, metal slicing against metal echoed against the brick walls.

A groan sounded beneath his boot as his heel connected with the downed man's head, and then he went silent. Madoc reached for his pistol but a blow to the gut sent him reeling against the building, He fought for breath. The swine rushed him, wrapping his great paws around Madoc's throat. The knife still in his hand, he drove it into the man's shoulder. As his attacker howled in pain and pulled at the blade, Madoc smashed his fist into the thug's bone-box and felt the teeth give way against his knuckles.

When the man stumbled back, Madoc withdrew his pistol and cocked it.

"Are we about ready for a drink, my friend," he said to Walters, panting and leaning a hand against the slippery brick. Every breath sent needles darting through his sides.

"Aye, these two have decided to take a nap. What shall we do with this last one?" Walters appeared at his side. "I didn't think it possible, but ye made the devil even uglier."

Madoc chuckled and then winced. Pain shot through his chest, like a blade between his ribs. The bloody devil cracked a rib or two. "Mill his canister and let's get out of here," he said with a grunt.

Walters approached the man. "I think ye have something belonging to us." He gripped the handle of the knife and yanked it from the man's shoulder. A howl of pain rang through the alley. As the man clutched his arm, Walters fist came up and caught the man's jaw. He crumpled to the ground.

"Are ye hurt bad, my lord?" asked Walters, wiping the blade on the unconscious man's jacket.

Madoc shook his head. "He battered a couple ribs but I've

had worse. Nothing that won't heal." He slid the gun back inside his coat, and they made their way back to the piazza. He'd have his man call a physician once he got back to his rooms. Wrapped up good and tight, he'd be fine and no one would be the wiser. He could hide the pain easily enough.

Walters hailed a hansom. "You don't need to walking all the way back, my lord. Let's get ye off your feet."

Once inside the cab, Madoc relaxed. "I'm afraid you'll have a bit of black and blue," he said of Walters' red and puffy eye. "I hate to say it, but I'll miss the occasional scuffle."

"There's always Gentleman Jackson's." Walters gingerly touched his eye. "I'm glad I saved the best news for last. I've located Caerton."

Madoc's pulse increased. Even if the money was never recovered, he wanted that swine brought to justice. Whether retribution came through the courts or otherwise, he didn't care. In fact, he preferred to take his own revenge.

When he'd first arrived in London, Walters had requested Madoc meet with a lad who was quick and talented at sketching. Madoc had described Caerton, and the boy had created a reasonable likeness for a penny. Walters had used it during his search, knowing the scoundrel had a new moniker.

"It seems our fugitive is more a chawbacon than clever embezzler. He's got a partner here in London who must be the brains behind this scheme. They were splitting the money, but Caerton found out his colleague was cheating him. I may have some information on the identity of the *associate* and checking on that presently."

Madoc finished his ale and beckoned to the barmaid. "Is Caerton still in Town?"

"Aye, and he's become quite the loose fish. Drinking, gambling. He's been high on the ropes, making a name for himself in the gaming hells. An ivory turner took him for a hundred pounds last week in a game of hazard. He's made himself known with the, er, ladies too. Dressed complete to a shade and spending coin on the finest trollops." Walters chuckled. "You won't like what he's calling himself."

Madoc pulled on the arm strap with a grunt and straightened. "Yes?"

"Mr. Griff Madoc." Walters leaned back in the chair, a grin on his ruddy face. "The man's got bollocks."

His half-brother's name and his own rolled into one. That bloody little louse. "It seems he's digging his own grave—with *my* money."

"Seems that way."

"Any ideas, besides a gun to the side of the man's head just for satisfaction?"

Another grin. "I have some comrades from Bow Street that are available for a price. They can befriend Caerton and gain his trust. Meet up with him at the tables. Let him win some, lose some, then—"

"How much?" Madoc mentally went through his ready, calculating how much he could spare.

"A pittance in advance, mind ye, but they'll take a percentage of the winnings for their wages. We can throw a rub Caerton's way."

"I'm listening."

CHAPTER TEN

"*P*apa, it's so good to have you home." Evelina threw her arms around his waist. "You must have arrived late last night."

Sir Horace smiled down at her. "We had a bit of trouble on the road, and I didn't want to spend the night in another strange bed. So, I hired another coach and rattled all the servants with my midnight entrance."

"Where is Mama?" She busied herself at the side table, filling a plate with toast, butter, and preserves. "Coffee?"

"Yes, please." He sat at the head of the table and tucked a napkin in his cravat. "Your mother was… tired. She's sleeping in this morning."

"How were the roads? You said you had business on your return trip." She poured coffee for her father and tea for herself, then passed the sugar.

"Excellent, though the ship ran into some bad weather and was late to dock. I tell you, Evie, there is nothing quite as satisfying as the completion of a profitable venture. And Fenella is comfortably settled with your grandmother." He added a lump of sugar to his cup. "How goes the Season during my absence? I assume there will be a dozen dandies asking for your hand by the end of the week?"

She giggled. "No. I have made several friends of the female persuasion, which has helped immensely with Fenella's absence. Grace, er, Lady Sunderland is the loveliest person. She and the earl went to the theater with Mama and Lord Brecken and I." Evie licked the spoon with the sticky jam, then wagged it at her father. "However, I'm not interested in a beau this season. I've decided it's like shopping with Mama at one of the bazaars. I'll inspect the goods first and then decide what deserves a second look."

Sir Horace set down his cup. "Evelina, don't refuse an offer for any reason other than you don't like a man. Don't turn down a proposal to be a martyr in your sister's name. It won't make either of you happy." He stuck his fork into a sausage. "For all we know, she could find love in Glasgow and never return to London."

Evie's hand flew to her chest, panic stealing her breath. "How can you say that? Fenella belongs here, with us, in London. She's like your partner in Franklin & Sons."

Her father reached over and squeezed her hand. There were more streaks of silver in his white-blond hair. "No, my dear, Fenella belongs wherever she's happiest. As do you. Where that may take either of my daughters, I have yet to see."

She took a deep breath and another. Papa was right. They were both adults now, and their paths were bound to lead in different directions. Better to prepare herself for the inevitable now.

"Have you written your sister recently? I understand you've been busy with one of the suitors you *aren't* interested in." Sir Horace returned his attention to the eggs, dipping his toast in the runny yolk. "Soirees, carriage rides, the theater?"

"I'm sure you'll meet Lord Brecken soon enough. I do

hope you like him, Papa." What if he didn't? How could she continue giving pieces of her heart to a man her father didn't like?

"If you think he's gentleman, and worthy of your time, I'm sure I'll agree." He popped the last bite of runny egg into his mouth and smacked his lips. "By the way, your grandmother sold the bookstore."

"What? She loved that shop." Had the world gone to sixes and sevens?

"She was tired and got a good price for it. Now she can enjoy the rest of her years and travel some. I believe she longs to see the Highlands again." Sir Horace rose and snapped his waistcoat down over his slight belly. "I believe I'm ready for the office. Your mother informed me there is a ball tonight. I shall see you at dusk."

Evelina returned to her rooms and settled at her writing table. She waved the feather back and forth, deciding what to put in her letter. The first two correspondences had been full of woe, how much she would miss her sister, how dreadful it was not to spend every day with her. She hadn't mentioned Lord Brecken at all. This time, Evie would weave him into the letter, just a remark here and there.

Dearest Fenella,

First, I must apologize for such sparse correspondence. Mama and I have been so busy. I have met several young ladies of good quality, as Mama puts it, and we've become fast friends. They help fill the void you left behind.

I must admit, I did not realize how much I depended on you. The first few weeks, I found myself going to your room to share something or ask your opinion. I was terribly lonesome. My new friends keep me company and ease the emptiness while you are away.

Now, on to news of London. I attended my first crush. It is aptly named as I could barely move through a room. However, Lord Brecken showed me how to move through a crowd with only my back brushing against another. The secret is to keep my fan a distance from my chest and walk sidelong, allowing for space to the front. It helps one to breathe and not succumb to the terrible heat.

One of those insipid girls who was unkind to you had a glass of punch spilled down her front. I do not know for certain how it happened, but the earl was nearby, and I'd just told him at the last musicale how horrid she was. I am certain there is a rascal hidden behind his perfect manners.

I have decided I quite like the theater. Lord Brecken has escorted Mama and I and promised to do so again. He has his own box for the season, and I wanted to pinch Mama when she continued to gush about it. I find him to be quite attentive and a perfect gentleman, though he's terribly old. Nearly six and twenty!

Evie realized the earl's name peppered the letter. Guilt flooded her. Perhaps her father was right, but old habits were hard to break. She dipped the nub into the inkwell again.

Oh my, rereading this, I see I have mentioned his name several times. Do not let your imagination run away with you. I have no designs on the earl. There are plenty of others who find his dark looks appealing. A competition does not interest me. He is merely a diversion until you return. I find he is quite useful in honing my skill of flirtation and quick wit. The gentleman is awake on every suit, and our conversations can be quite lively. Did I mention he is also an accomplished dancer?

I hope you are not too bored in Glasgow. Why on earth did Grandmama sell the bookstore without informing us? Of course, she was the owner and certainly doesn't need our approval. I shall

miss the dusty old place. And I miss you dreadfully. Give Grand-
mama a hug and a kiss for me. Papa sends both to you. He's never
been much for writing, but reminded me to send salutations.
Enclosed is also a letter from Mama.

Your devoted sister,

Evie

Madoc scanned the ballroom. He was late, but the meeting
with his superior had gone better than expected. He'd delivered the report and, as Walters predicted, was finally released
from duty. For now. The Home Office never completely let a
man go, and one always had to be prepared to help his country. He'd also met the older gentleman who would be
working with Walters and was pleased with the outcome. As
far as Caerton and the stolen inheritance… They were within
ames-ace. So very close.

The event was crowded, but not the same crush they'd
attended last week. He'd come close to kissing her then, out
on the balcony, under the stars, a cool breeze ruffling the
curls against her cheeks. Madoc knew he should continue his
search for an heiress. Miss Evelina might not have sizeable
dowry he needed. Caerton may have only a pocketful of
coins left. Yet, those alluring brandy eyes refused to let him
go. He was obsessed with everything about her.

The way her eyes sparkled when she thought she was
clever. The husky tone when she confided something. The
satisfaction that enveloped his heart when he amused her,
the sweet peal of laughter that tickled his ears. Her lips as
they turned up in a slow smile. The long, silken curls of

caramel that he wanted to slide his fingers through. The hollow of her throat that begged his lips to... *Blast and perdition! Don't go down that road now.*

In a corner of the room, a tall man guffawed, the sound carrying over the many voices in the room. He was close to his own father's age with pale blond hair and streaks of silver. He seemed familiar, and his expensive black suit of clothes and ruby cravat pin indicated wealth. Then the lady always foremost in his mind appeared by his side, and he knew who the stranger reminded him of. *Fenella!* She was the image of her father. As the baronet stepped away, Doc saw Lady Franklin. Yes, it was Sir Horace Franklin.

His attention returned to the striking beauty next to him. Miss Evelina wore a low-cut satin gown of pale gold with a delicate emerald overlay that glistened and came alive each time she moved. Amber tresses had been braided and wrapped around her head like a ribbon, with tiny gems of topaz and emerald giving her a halo effect. The rest of her tawny locks were swept up at the crown and cascaded onto her neck. When she laughed at something her father said, her bare shoulders shook gently, showing off her creamy bosom. The blood pulsed in his temple and shot through to his core. The woman was breathtaking.

"Good evening, Lord Brecken, how goes the hunt?" Brooks appeared at his elbow. "Any more contenders?"

He shook his head. "And you?"

"I think I've decided to be happy with my present circumstances." Brooks grunted. "Miss Wilkerson carries a pleasant enough conversation, knows the social graces, is pliant, and dotes on me. I believe we're well-suited."

Madoc snorted. "You make it sound so easy."

"It is, really, if you're not some mawkish romantic who must have love rather than a partnership." The baron's gaze followed Doc's across the room. "It seems Sir Horace hasn't mentioned the size of his second daughter's dowry. After a disastrous first season, my guess is the size of Miss Franklin's was alluded to in order to attract interest. Since Miss Evelina is so much more... A close friend of Sir Horace's told me he was waiting to see who was interested. The amount would depend on the suitor."

"That's as helpful as a lame horse." So, Madoc would have to make his intentions known to find out the dowry. What if it wasn't enough? He couldn't back out once he'd spoken to Miss Evelina's father. He was effectively hobbled.

"I can tell you that Sir Horace is an honorable man and very fond of his daughters. I believe if he likes you, and trusts your affection for his daughter, he would offer the same generous amount he did for the elder." They watched Mrs. Wilkerson by the refreshment table, flapping her fleshy arms in their direction. Her frizzy brown curls were mostly tucked into a puce turban that matched her tight gown. "I've been summoned. Good luck, Doc, and let me know how it goes."

He sucked in a deep breath, tossed back the champagne, and grabbed another from a passing tray as he ambled toward the Franklins. The knot in his stomach twisted and tightened at the thought of losing Miss Evelina. As did the idea of breaking her heart. If Madoc were to transfer his attentions elsewhere, she would be confused and feel betrayed. He couldn't blame her, and he'd only have himself to blame. The chit had worked her way under his skin, and the thought of marriage with another left a sour taste in his mouth.

Studying her father, he decided this would be a night of reconnaissance. Tomorrow he'd plan his next step.

"Lord Brecken, its lovely to see you again," cooed Lady Franklin. "May I introduce my husband, Sir Horace Franklin. My dear, this is the Earl of Brecken."

Sir Horace's smile was warm and his handshake firm.

"Thank you for keeping my girls entertained while I was away. They speak highly of you."

Doc gave Miss Evelina a sideways glance. She studied her gold leather shoes, a tinge of pink coloring her cheeks. But when she looked up at him with those soft brown eyes, a slight smile turning up her full, pink lips, he shared the heat from his belly to his neck. She always had the same effect on him. Always the same need when he was near her.

"I'm relieved to hear it, Sir Horace. And your reputation precedes you, sir. If I remember correctly, you were known as the Merlin of hard-to-find goods during the war."

"I'm a resourceful man," admitted Sir Horace.

"And stubborn," added Lady Franklin. "I believe that's the secret to his success."

"It's why you married me, my sweet. I wouldn't take 'no' for an answer."

Madoc turned to Miss Evelina. "This is much better than the crush we attended, don't you think? I went home smelling like half of London last week."

She laughed. "Yes, it's certainly an improvement. Could you imagine trying to dance?"

"A crush is not for dancing, my dear," explained Lady Franklin. "It's to see and be seen. The more people, the higher one's popularity. I do find them tiresome, though."

"Speaking of dances, please save one for me," he said to Evelina.

"Only if it's a waltz. I need to wash away the memory of the last one," she quipped. "My feet have suffered terribly for Lord Hempton's overindulgence of ratafia."

"I can't believe the old sop can still dance," joked her father. "Consider yourself lucky he didn't topple over on you."

"I'll do my best to erase the unpleasant memory from your mind," added Madoc gallantly. He joined in more small talk, waiting an appropriate amount of time before asking, "Would you care for a promenade, Miss Evelina?"

They strolled the perimeter of the room, enjoying the open windows and light breeze that stirred the air inside. When they reached the terrace that led to the garden, she stopped. "A walk in the moonlight would be divine tonight."

She peeked at him through her dark lashes, and a wave of desire ignited low in his belly. He opened his mouth to answer but was saved by the orchestra. "You'll appreciate the breeze so much more afterwards. Shall we?" He turned on his heel in the opposite direction and offered her his other arm. "Have I told you how stunning you look?"

"Yes, but feel free to repeat it as often as you like." She gave him a dazzling smile and held her gloved hand up, waiting for him.

He placed one hand on the small of her back and held her as close as he dared, his other cradling her palm against his. She fit him like his favorite leather hunting gloves. Soft and pliable, clinging yet not constrictive.

It would be torture to let her go, then see her in the arms of another. For the first time is years, he said a silent prayer as he pulled her into a sweeping turn.

CHAPTER ELEVEN

*H*e smelled of soap and leather and the woods. Ambergris, perhaps? She'd never considered the scent heavenly until she met Lord Brecken. It would forever remind her of the man who was becoming such a dominant part of her life. In barely two months, Evie couldn't fathom a day without at least a mention of Lord Brecken. They drove in Hyde Park on Tuesdays and attended a minimum of two evening activities weekly.

If your father was home, he'd ask for your hand. I'm sure of it, Mama had said a few days before Papa returned.

Evie closed her eyes, lifted her face to the waft of air as the earl spun them in a half circle and then another. Her head only came to the top of his navy waistcoat, and she imagined being lifted into his arms as easily as hoisting a saddle. The muscles flexed in his broad shoulders as he dipped and swirled her about the floor. Would her stomach ever grow used to his body close to hers? Would her heart ever stop racing when he just entered a room? According to Lady Sunderland, Evie had all the symptoms of Cupid's malady. It was a heady sensation, this falling in love.

The final notes faded, and she stood half-panting, one hand covering her chest. "Now would be a good time for that walk," he whispered in her ear.

His breath skimmed her lobe, and a tightness pulsed low in her core. With shaking fingers, she gripped his arm and followed him through the clusters of guests. He'd been right about waiting for the stroll. The night air dried her damp skin. She leaned on him as they descended the shallow steps to the garden, the exertion from the dance and his proximity making her legs unsteady.

"I imagine you are glad to have Sir Horace back home?" he asked. "Especially with your sister also gone."

"I missed him terribly. So did Mama, though she's loath to admit it." Her thin overlay brushed a rose bush and caught. She stopped, releasing Lord Brecken's arm and found the offending thorn. "Pish and petunias, I've torn it."

He bent to inspect the sheer material and rubbed it between his thumb and fingers. His knuckles brushed her calf. Her breath caught, and his hand stilled. He dropped the skirt slowly, his fingertips grazing her thigh as his gaze lifted to the rise and fall of her chest, the pulse pounding in her neck, and finally her face. Straightening, his eyes locked on her lips. With the pad of his thumb, he stroked her mouth. The rough skin, the gentle touch, sent searing flames through her.

"Do you have any idea how beautiful you are?" he asked, his eyes still on her mouth.

Evie shook her head; her breath quickened. *Oh, heavens, he's going to kiss me.*

Lord Brecken moved his hand to cradle her cheek, his thumb now caressing her temple, and a whimper escaped her throat. He chuckled. "Confound it, you were made for love, Evie," he rasped.

Was he angry? But he'd said her name—her given name—as if it were a word of passion.

He bent his head and brushed her lips with his, the barest touch, once, twice. Like she would dip her toe in the ocean at Bath to test the waters. A shiver passed over her, then his mouth covered hers, and the world went topsy-turvy. She closed her eyes and gave in to her body, gave in to her own desire. And found that her dreams couldn't compare to the man. His lips were velvet, just as she knew they would be. The edge of his beard tickled her chin, and she breathed in his spicy scent. His hand came away from her face, his arms went around her, and his body pressed against hers. He was hardness and muscle and power.

Evie wanted to drown in the sensations that tore through her body. Her arms moved of their own accord and wrapped around his neck. His hair was thick and silky beneath her touch, his skin like tanned leather, soft yet strong. When his tongue traced her lips, Evie instinctively parted them and allowed his tongue to dart in, then out. Never had she felt anything like this. It was as if a stormy ocean tossed and turned within her, crashing and receding.

His fingers tangled in her hair, then tilted her head back, and his lips left a trail of fire down her neck. Her chest heaved, her hands clutched his shoulders to stay upright on legs that had turned to jelly. And then his mouth was gone, her skin was cold again, and she opened her eyes.

Lord Brecken shook his head, vibrant green sparking in his hazel eyes. "I'm so sorry, Miss Evelina. I shouldn't have done that. I have no right—"

She grabbed the lapels of his coat, pushed up on her tiptoes, and kissed him again. "You have every right, my lord. And I prefer Evie."

. . .

***

The night had been pure torture. Miss Evelina—Evie—had been everything he'd imagined. Soft, pliant, smelling of sweet lavender, and oh, so willing. Each time he dozed, she emerged behind his lids, teasing and laughing. Madoc rose from the four-poster, resigned to a sleepless night. He went to the writing table but found only a few sheets of paper.

His rooms and the service at the Wicked Earls' Club were sumptuous. His toes sank into the lush carpet beneath his bare feet, shadows from the oil lamp gleamed against paneled walls, satin bed linens covered multiple feather ticks, and his favorite French brandy was stocked in the liquor cabinet. With the pull of a rope, he could request any craving at any time. Need a discreet bit of muslin? Done. Extra protection for an expedition to one of London's seedier districts? Done. A keg of smuggled, untaxed brandy? Done. The butler might be offended when asked to procure only writing pen, paper, and a bottle of ink.

Lady Brecken had written, informing him that renovations were underway, and Griff had sent over a candidate for estate manager. She needed him home. He was torn, not wanting to leave Miss Evelina. With a ragged sigh, he ran a hand through his hair and flopped back against the chair. Brooks' comment went round in his head.

I can tell you that Sir Horace is an honorable man and very fond of his daughters. I believe if he likes you, and trusts your affection for his daughter, he would offer the same generous amount he did for the elder.

If that were true, he needed time to earn his confidence. No toad-eating flummery, just honesty. Once he was sure Sir Horace favored him, he would broach the subject of a betrothal to Miss Evelina. He would delay his return to

Brecken Castle until June. Hopefully, he would have news for Mama concerning his marriage prospects.

***

Evie sat in her window seat, watching for Lord Brecken's carriage. He, Brooks, and the Wilkersons would be dinner guests tonight. She was growing fond of Lavinia. The two formed a tentative friendship when Evelina had found the girl sobbing in the necessity room at a dance. Lavinia had heard some of her "friends" making fun of her and Lord Brooks. Evie's heart had gone out to the girl, when she'd blurted, *They said we'd have the ugliest babies in the whole of London. I can't have a child as bracket-faced as I am.*

Evelina had assured her that a mother always sees the beauty in their children, and those girls had been jealous. She may not have believed Evie, but her loyalty had been fixed from that moment on. Mama had been right. Insecurities had led Lavinia to go along with the cruel jokes and gossip of the other girls. She'd only wanted to belong. Fenella would find a friend in Miss Wilkerson when she returned.

But it was also Tuesday, and she and the earl would drive in Hyde Park this afternoon before the evening event. It was a cloudy May afternoon, and she crossed her fingers it wouldn't rain. When Lord Brecken arrived, the first wet plops of rain splashed the window panes. He dashed up the front steps, pounding the iron ring on the door. The butler gave him entrance, and her father met them both in the portico.

"I think you need an alternate plan, Lord Brecken," said Sir Horace amiably as the earl brushed the droplets from shoulders and beaver hat.

"Perhaps it will"—thunder rumbled—"stop," Evie finished.

Lord Brecken stood, holding his wet hat, his brows furrowed with indecision. "We could…"

"Chess," exclaimed Sir Horace. "Do you play, Lord Brecken?"

"I do, sir," he answered, relief in his tone.

"Well, then, who shall challenge him first, my dear?"

"Oh, I believe you should rout him thoroughly, Papa. It will be monstrous fun to watch."

"Thank you for your confidence, Miss Evelina," said Lord Brecken, a smirk bringing out his dimple.

She and Lady Franklin embroidered while the two men played. It began with polite exchanges until more and more ivory pieces were removed from the board. Good-natured jibes were added to the polite conversation each time one of them gained advantage with a move.

"Think you're clever, eh? Young malapert!" jested Sir Horace.

"Don't threaten me, you old termagant," retorted Brecken.

Evie laughed. "You two sound like an old married couple!"

"You know he enjoys a good bashing, my lord," added Lady Franklin.

"As did my father." Lord Brecken smiled and tipped his head at Sir Horace. "I thank you for reviving those memories regardless of the outcome."

In that moment, Evie saw glimpses of a future with the earl. Her father liked him. Their immediate rapport was obvious. Sir Horace would embrace his sons-in-law as only a man with no sons can. The earl missed his own father.

"Check," announced Lord Brecken. He sat back against the velvet cushion, his fingertips resting on the lip of the carved chess board.

Silence hung heavy over the room as Sir Horace glowered at the board, a finger pressed to his lips. Her father had a jovial personality but also a competitive side. He didn't like to lose in business, chess, or horse racing. He picked up his king, then set it back down with a grunt. He picked his knight and did the same.

"I can't move, blast you!" he mumbled.

"You mentioned my first born, Sir Horace. Since I'm the victor, I'd prefer your second born." Lord Brecken winked at Evie, and her father burst out laughing.

"Save me the headache and cost of a wedding, and she's yours!"

The smile fell from the earl's face. He cleared his throat and rose from the table, adjusting his cravat and avoiding eye contact with Evie. She didn't know what to make of it. Was it the mention of marriage to her? Or the mention of the institution in general? Or the fact that he'd beaten her father at chess? The memory of their kiss flooded back, and she decided on the latter.

"The rain has stopped. Shall we go for a walk in the garden?" she asked, anxious to talk to Lord Brecken and ease her mind.

"The purple delphiniums are in bloom, and the pink are just beginning," informed Lady Franklin. "Take a basket and shears and cut some, please. They're so pretty for dried arrangements."

Evie collected a basket and shears from the kitchen. Lord Brecken looped his forearm through the wicker handle and offered her the other. As they strolled the main path, she looked over her shoulder to see her father watching them from the parlor window.

"I feel eyes upon us." Lord Brecken whispered loudly, a hand over one side of his mouth. "Please, I beg you, don't take advantage of me now. I'll be ruined."

She giggled and stopped at one of the tall stems with the tiny purple blooms. "I wish these had a scent, but Mama is right. They are lovely."

"The most fetching in London."

Evie glanced up and found he was staring at her rather than the flowers. "Thank you," she murmured, her cheeks hot. "Can I ask you something?"

"Certainly," he answered, holding out the basket for the clippings.

"Why did you turn serious when Papa mentioned me and weddings?"

He sighed. "Because I must return to Wales. There is work to be done that I need to oversee, and a steward needs to be hired." He stopped and turned to face her. "I received a letter from my mother, requesting I come home."

She pulled in air, realizing she'd been holding her breath waiting for his answer. "How long will you be gone?"

"I'll leave at the end of the month." He ran a hand through his dark hair. "I can't ask you to wait for me. I doubt I'm back before the end of the season."

Fear gripped her chest, and she struggled for composure. She had thought a proposal was around the corner, and now he would be gone in a week. "But I thought... I thought we..." Her lips pressed together to hold back her denials. She had her pride, and if he could abandon her so easily, then he could... he could go to the devil.

"I wish my situation were different. We've been left in a precarious state without a steward, and I'm needed." He blew out a breath, his eyes pleading. "It's my duty, my inheritance. I have no choice, Miss Evelina. I would love nothing better than to stay here with you."

"When will you return?" she asked, taking comfort in the fact he didn't want to leave. She swallowed the lump in her throat and blinked back hot tears.

"As soon as humanly possible."

The answer soothed the mayhem in her belly. "Then I *will* wait, of course."

"But Miss Evelina—"

"I would think you know me well enough by now. Once I've made up my mind, I don't waver. I'm like my father in that way." She crossed her arms defiantly. "If you argue with me, I'll throw my arms around you and kiss you while my father is watching."

A smile tugged at her lips as the panic flashed across his face. "Now you're being reasonable," she said smugly before continuing down the path. "Oh, here's Solomon's seal."

They moved toward the next plant, and she pointed to the tiny white buds. "They look like little bells," remarked the earl.

"Yes, Grandmama says if you listen closely you can hear them tinkle." She bent down, placed her finger under a row of the blossoms, and tapped them. "Can you hear it?"

He shook his head and bent down, one ear toward the plant.

"Closer."

He bent farther, his face positioned within reach. Evie leaned forward and kissed his cheek, then stilled. He turned and their lips brushed. The earl let slip a husky moan, and a hand cupped her cheek. His mouth covered hers, caressing her lips with his. She closed her eyes as the familiar spin of her belly caused havoc with her sense.

"You are a temptress, Miss Evelina," he growled, then straightened. "You don't realize your effect on me."

"I said I prefer Evie." With that, she turned on her heel, strode into the house, and left Lord Brecken holding the basket of clipped, purple delphiniums.

CHAPTER TWELVE

*T*hree days. He had three more days to find out the amount of Miss Evelina's dowry. Madoc stood in the dining room of White's, pondering his next move. Sir Horace sat alone at a table, reading the Times and sipping port. *Now or never, you coward*, he prodded himself.

Madoc eased into the chair beside Sir Horace and cleared his throat. A snap of a newspaper, and Sir Horace's silver-streaked blond hair came into view.

"Good evening, Lord Brecken."

"Good evening, sir." Madoc opened his mouth and closed it. His mind had gone blank, the practiced inquiry forgotten. He struggled to find words.

"Did you wish to speak with me?"

Doc nodded, his mind whirling with several different approaches. "If it's not a good time…"

"Why don't we go into the library where it's more private?" suggested Sir Horace.

"Thank you," he agreed with a loud sigh. It bought him a few more minutes to sound like a man with some sense rather than a muddleheaded green boy.

Once installed in the library, a glass of port in their hand, both men studied the orange and yellow flames. "I'll be blunt. My daughter is quite taken with you, my lord. Is the affection returned?" It was a simple statement. Madoc wished he had a simple answer.

"She's a beautiful lady."

"That's not what I asked."

"No, it wasn't." Madoc swirled the deep ruby liquid. "I have responsibilities."

"We all do," Sir Horace agreed patiently. He set down his glass and folded his hands across his stomach, his full attention on the earl.

"What are your intentions? Do you care for my daughter?"

"I do."

"Are you considering marriage in the near future?"

"I am."

"You realize I'm not a dentist?"

"Yes." Madoc scowled at the fiery embers, wondering where this was leading.

"Yet extracting words from you is like pulling a tooth."

Doc glanced up to see Sir Horace smiling. "I love her, Sir Horace," he blurted out.

Where did that come from? Did he love her? Yes, you lecherous lickpenny! The silent voice bounced in his brain.

"With all my heart," he finished lamely.

"A match between the two of you would make my wife very happy." Sir Horace picked up his glass and sipped his port. "I feel as if there is a sizeable secret hovering above us. It's about to break open like the storm the other day when you visited."

"I'm broke." It was out. "I'm here looking for a wife with a generous dowry. Instead, I fell in love with Miss Evelina."

"I'm not surprised after the kiss in the garden. But you said, *instead*. You must know I'm quite plump in the pocket. Or is it our social status?"

Embarrassment spread up his neck as he shook his head. He could feel the sweat popping out on his brow and resisted the urge to wipe it away. "She doesn't know about my financial situation. Miss Evelina should be courted by a man who will love her for who she is, not for the dowry she will bring. Yet, here I am caught to Point non-Plus, wanting her for the woman she is but trapped by my obligations to find a wealthy wife."

"You realize you are just what Lady Franklin has been looking for to elevate her social status? A penniless aristocrat willing to marry below his class. My wife rattles on about your ancient family lines and title. It wouldn't make a difference to her." Sir Horace took another sip, his eyes narrowed as he studied Madoc. "Tell me your circumstances."

For the next hour, Madoc talked. He recounted his life from the time of his father's accident, omitting his work for the Home Office. "And that leads us to the present."

Sir Horace nodded and poured another brandy. "Interesting story. I can put out some inquiries about Caerton myself. I have connections in all the nooks and crannies of London. My first office was on the docks."

"I'd appreciate that." The fist in Madoc's chest loosened. The man didn't seem fazed by his circumstances.

"How much?"

The abruptness of the question caught him unaware. "Pardon me?"

"How much were you hoping for as a dowry?" Sir Horace's steely gaze pinned Madoc. "And where would you live?"

"The amount rumored for your oldest daughter would be

ample." He swallowed, his stomach roiling as he haggled for Miss Evelina like a horse at Tattersall's. Madoc held up his hand, palm out. "I can't do this. She deserves someone who doesn't need her money."

"She deserves to be happy and loved. Both my daughters do. Our goal here is to determine if you can provide both. If so, the cost is inconsequential." Sir Horace smiled. "I am a very wealthy man. If I can't make my girls' dreams come true, what use is it to me?"

Madoc blinked. A man with scruples who didn't use his daughters to further his connections. "I would do everything in my power to do both, sir. But standing at this crossroad, I realize I'm unable to go through with it. It would hang over our heads and darken our marriage. She would always wonder if I truly loved her."

Sir Horace nodded. "I can understand that. As a business-man, giving money away doesn't rub me well. Yet, marriage and contracts and dowries are part of life. My wife says it's an investment in our future. Our daughters' future, anyway."

Both men returned their gaze to the fire and sipped their brandy. Madoc clenched his jaw, thinking of the confession he'd just made. He loved Miss Evelina Franklin. "I can't turn my back on my responsibilities, but I don't want to lose your daughter."

"Would you consider a loan?" Sir Horace leaned forward.

"Absolutely not." The idea of owing his future father-in-law appalled him.

"You aren't making this easy, my lord. You love my daughter. I believe you'll make her happy. You have integrity and honor and are attempting to restore your family seat." He pursed his mouth and wagged a finger at Madoc. "If the boot were on the other foot, would you still offer for her?"

"Within a heartbeat."

"Then let me help you."

An idea sparked in Madoc's brain. "Would you consider… No, never mind." It was unfair to ask. "You're a busy man."

"Go on, spit it out now that you've started."

"Would you consider coming to Brecken Castle? I could show you my lands, and you would better understand my predicament. We would both enter this agreement with eyes wide open. You'll know if Miss Evelina would be content there. I'm not opposed to spending part of my time in London, either. I'd like to resume the seat my father neglected in the House of Lords," he admitted.

Sir Horace brightened. "I'll be in your neck of the country in July. Taking the boat from Bristol over to Cardiff. I could ride up to Brecknock after I conclude my business. Would that suit you?"

He nodded. "Yes. Yes, it would suit me fine. If you're still confident I'll make her a good husband, it would be my honor to propose upon our return. To ease my conscience, I will add her original dowry price to the widow's jointure we agree upon."

"And we won't mention this to my daughter until I've seen the estate, and it's settled. Will you agree to that?"

"It's more than fair."

"Until we meet at Brecken Castle, then?" Sir Horace stood and held out his hand.

Madoc gave him a hearty shake. His heartbeat slowed, the fist around it unclenched. A glimmer of hope surged through him, and he snatched the slender the thread. His lifeline for the next month.

***

. . .

"Evie," he whispered in her hair as she leaned against him. They were in the Franklin's garden, under a tree in the shadows. The stars glittered above them, the night air was warm, and her soft, pliant body melded into his like the last puzzle piece. "We should go in. We've been out too long as it is."

"I won't see you for months!" She twisted in his arms and faced him, her palms on each of his cheeks. "Who will I flirt with while you're gone?"

His jaws clenched at the thought of her smiling up at another man. "Brooks is the only one I'll allow."

"Gah! You have no claim on me, sir. I shall dally with whoever I choose." She leaned up on her tiptoes and kissed his chin. One finger circled his dimple.

He closed his eyes. How could he explain? Resigned, he nuzzled her neck, breathing in the sweet lavender and wondering how he would hide his reaction to her backside wiggling against him. She had no idea how naïve she really was.

"I have some matters to attend in Wales, and when I return, we will discuss... things."

"Things? I'm a *thing*?"

He stopped his ministrations on her neck and cradled her face in his palms. "The most delectable, beautiful, alluring thing in the county."

"Only the county?"

"In all of England." He chuckled and brushed her lips. "Are you satisfied?"

"For now," she purred.

He wrapped his arms around her and held her close, burying his nose in her satin hair. Her arms snaked around his shoulders, tickling the back of his neck as finger softly caressed his skin. Blast! It would seem like a lifetime without her. Is that what love did to a person? It drove him mad when she wasn't near, within eyesight to make him feel whole and content. Would he survive, live on if he couldn't have her? Yes. But he knew with an unexplainable certainty that he would never love another woman as he did Miss Evelina Franklin.

***

I'm in love. Evie hugged herself and twirled around until she was dizzy. She had to write her sister. Fenella was working as an accountant for a factory in Glasgow. It was owned by the MacNaughton clan, and she'd mentioned the name Lachlan more than several times in her letters. Perhaps her dear sister had found love too. She giggled. Their mother would have an apoplexy if her eldest daughter married a Scot. Lady Franklin had worked most of her life to erase her Scottish heritage.

Evie had confided in Papa about her feelings for Lord Brecken. His advice had been to be patient and all would work out as it should. As if she'd leave anything to fate.

Madoc! When he returned, he would propose, and she would call him Madoc. What a virile name. It felt decadent rolling off her tongue.

Would he bring Lady Brecken with him? What if his mother didn't like her? What if she was one of those women who felt no woman was good enough for her son? *Stop counting those eggs!* she scolded.

Lady Franklin knocked on her door. "May I come in?"

"Of course, Mama. I was just daydreaming." She fell back on the counterpanes, sinking into the mattresses, her arms over her head. "I'm so happy!"

"Well, save some of that buoyancy for the actual proposal. But I have no doubt it will come." She smiled like the cat who'd finally trapped the mouse. "Your father seems confident this match will come to fruition. He rarely makes a prediction unless the odds are in his favor."

CHAPTER THIRTEEN

July 1819
Brecken Castle, Wales

*M*adoc wiped the sweat from his brow and let out a long, loud satisfied sigh. He'd insisted on helping with the raising bee. There was a certain satisfaction knowing he'd helped build the barn that would house many of the tenants' livestock. The main street of the village had improved. While there was still work to do, cursory repairs had been made, and Brecknock was once again tidy and inviting. He examined the buildings and St. Mary's Church with pride. It was an ancient place, built by the Romans as their first military base when they invaded Wales.

The village had given him a hearty welcome with a bonfire and slaughtered two pigs for a much-deserved celebratory feast. The perfect end to a terrible ordeal. Too much ale, too much wine, too much whisky, too much food. They had hailed him as a hero for taking care of his responsibilities. For doing what never should have *needed* to be done. They were good people, and he was blessed.

"You've done a fine job, Brecken," said Sir Horace, accepting a cup of cool water from a lad with a bucket. "Your tenants are loyal and hardworking, just like their master."

"I'd say we didn't need your help, sir, but it was much appreciated. You're very fit for..." *Blast!* How did he finish that sentence?

"A man my age? Well, I do a little boxing, hunting, and ride every day. I've always liked the satisfaction of a job done well." He dipped the wooden cup back into the bucket and gulped it down. "I've helped unload my own shipments countless times. There's something about physical labor that makes a man feel like a man, don't you agree?"

"I do." Madoc had grown close to his future father-in-law over the past weeks. He was a shrewd man with a keen eye, quick wit, and kind heart. For Madoc, Sir Horace helped replace that void left by his father so many years ago. For Franklin, a man who loved daughters fiercely, the earl was a way to embrace a son.

"I'll be leaving tomorrow." Sir Horace nodded at the blacksmith as he passed. "I miss my wife and my daily routine."

"My mother has been happy to have your company in the evenings. Her winnings from your nightly games of loo are embarrassingly large."

Sir Horace guffawed. "She's an excellent player. I'm glad she's not a man, or I'd have to lose to her at White's."

The men said their goodbyes and mounted their horses. Sir Horace pulled a flask from his coat, took a drink, and handed it to Madoc. He took a swallow and gave it back. "Good brandy, sir. My father always preferred whisky. Don't care for the stuff, myself."

"Nor I," said Franklin, studying Madoc. "I wasn't sure

what to expect when I arrived. Your mother is gracious and lovely. I presumed the lands and buildings would be much worse off than they are. It shows me two things."

Madoc nodded. "Go on."

"First, you've already poured your blood and sweat into this estate. It shows initiative and pride." Franklin tipped back the flask and passed it to Madoc again.

"And the second?" he asked before taking another swallow.

"You describe this place as ramshackle, deteriorated. In my eyes, it needs work, but it's not crumbling. This leads to me believe the estate must have been glorious to appear so decayed to you." Sir Horace tucked the flask inside his jacket. "I have every confidence my daughter will be well-loved and provided for. That makes me a very content papa."

The two me rode back to the castle in companionable silence.

Madoc's chest swelled. Words of praise that were deeply appreciated, especially from Evie's father. His mind wandered to Evie, as it always did these days.

What would she think of his lands, the castle, his inheritance? Would she love Wales as he did? The land and their location were remote, the winds often blustery and cold, the waters turbulent. Yet, he somehow knew that she would embrace this land and the people. She would be their countess, and the villagers would love her in return.

"Rub them down and give them extra oats. They worked hard today," he told the stableboy as they handed off their reins. The earl turned to Sir Horace. "We'll see you in the parlor before dinner?"

"Of course. And one more chance to lessen my losses. Tell Lady Brecken that a reckoning is coming."

Madoc took the steps two at a time and peeled his clothes off, dropping them on the floor of his chamber as he walked toward the bed. He was exhausted and satisfied. After a bath and a meal, he'd write Evie. She had been constant and merry with her correspondence, and with each mention of Lord Brooks, he'd relaxed. Madoc had asked his friend to watch over her. Sunderland and his wife had returned to the country in June. Grace was growing large, and Kit had been anxious to have her home. Most of the nobles escaped the heat and smells of London until the summer heat ended.

In the dining room, refreshed and hungry, he stuck his nose in the silver bowl of roasted fowl and inhaled the scent of spices and juices. His stomach growled.

"It seems you worked up an appetite," his mother said from the doorway. "Shall I pour you some wine?"

"Thank you. Sir Horace will be down shortly. I think he enjoyed the bee raising today."

"He seems like the type of man who would. Your father used to lend a hand the same way." She handed him the glass and poured herself some madeira. "With her father leaving tomorrow, I must ask when I will meet the famed Miss Evelina Franklin."

"I expect you'll return with me to London. Would you rather I arrange transport later?" He wondered if London intimidated Lady Brecken. Or if she would be jealous of his young wife and resent becoming the dowager countess. He'd heard horrific stories of mothers and new wives in a constant battle of hierarchy. Yet, this had been her idea.

"I shall accompany you. I'd like to know the entire family. Will she live here? It's a far cry from Town." She nodded at the servant who began ladling out a clear broth. "Will she be bored?"

"Does it matter? You wanted me to find a wife with a large dowry. I did. I will expect you to treat her as a daughter and help her acclimate to her new surroundings." He finished the broth in three swallows, discarding the spoon and tipping the bowl to his mouth.

"Of course it matters. And why would I treat her badly? I'm looking forward to another woman to share my afternoons." She sipped the broth without a slurp. "When will you tell her about our... situation?"

"I don't know. When the time is right," he answered irritably. "Let's take one step at a time."

"She must know before the ceremony. You cannot begin a new life with her on a lie."

"Yes, I realize that," he said with gritted teeth. "I will know when the time is right. But first, I will propose."

"Shouldn't you tell her before she accepts?"

"I've done as you asked, was fortunate enough to find a woman I care for, so I believe I've proven myself capable. I will tell her when I deem it appropriate and not sooner." He threw back his wine, swallowing loudly. "The subject is closed."

"You've been rubbing elbows with the tenants too long," his mother admonished. "Mind your manners in front of your future father-in-law."

"I'm not worried about my manners with Sir Horace. He's more concerned with his daughter's happiness."

"I wish my father had been."

Madoc paused. His mother's upbringing had been so different. As a female, she'd been a pawn among men, a brood mare for a Welsh earl. He reached over and squeezed her hand. He couldn't imagine Evelina being forced to marry a man she'd never even met. "I wish he had been too. I'm glad you met my father and found happiness."

He heard his voice. He heard the patronizing tone and winced. Yet, he couldn't help himself. After the late earl's accident, his mother had almost... forgotten him. She had spoken harshly without provocation, shushed him when he asked about his father's condition. He hadn't been allowed to be angry or sad or confused. He knew that young boy's anger had not been dispelled.

"Why did you ignore me after Father's accident?"

Her spoon dropped into her soup bowl. "I beg your pardon?"

"After Father's accident, everything centered around him. It was like I no longer existed. Do you have any idea what that felt like to a fifteen-year-old boy?" He leaned his elbows on the table. "First, I lost my father and then my mother abandoned me, through no fault of my own. I had no hero to look up to and no comfort from the woman who had once doted on me. It was as if his crippled legs had sucked up all the happiness in my family."

"Is that what you thought?" A hand covered her mouth. "I always loved you, Madoc."

"I didn't understand that."

"I know I was harsh with you after the accident. First, he was horrified at what he'd become and didn't want anyone but his manservant and the physician to see him. It wasn't just the walking, it was the fact he had to rely on others for simple things. He no longer felt capable of being a man. He gave up.

"Stoicism became his defense. He would look at some point across the room, never blinking, as if in a trance, while he was bathed and ministered to each day. Each bath, each emptying of a chamber pot, each night I when we lay together and nothing else…" Her cheeks pinkened and she looked away. "I was petrified. He was my life, my love, my heart. He had made my life not only bearable but wonderful. Who would take care of me?"

Madoc stilled. His mother had rarely spoken of the early years of his father's infirmity.

"When he allowed me back in, I spent every moment I could with him. Our daily conversations became my motivation. For an hour or two each day, he was the man I married. We reminisced of good times, of memories that might make him see life as valuable again, even without the use of his legs. I was single-minded in my determination, and that's what you remember most, I think. But I had to be strong, be iron-willed to hang on until he got over his bitterness. And I would be there."

"I always thought you loved him more than me." He hated the accusation in his voice. The needling tone of a wounded youth.

"You were my purpose in life—but he *was* my life. Without him, I am half-empty and will wither away. So yes, he was my priority from the day of the accident until he took his last breath." She blinked, tears spilling down her cheeks. "Now, we must fulfill our promise. I cannot join him until that is done."

"Mama, don't talk like that." He was shocked. His mother wasn't old enough to give up on life and join her husband. "I still need you."

She stood and walked to him with her arms extended. "Oh, my poor, sweet boy. I do love you so."

Madoc stood and enfolded her in a tight hug.

"I'm not going anywhere yet, but you must be prepared," she murmured into his chest. "Life without him is too hard. I just don't have the strength."

***

July 1819
London

"Lord Raines, it's so good to see you again." Evelina had caught a glimpse of the tall blond after the last dance set.

"Lord Brooks, Miss Wilkerson, this is Viscount Raines, a friend of my cousin Charles."

"It's a pleasure," welcomed Lavinia.

"I believe we met once." Brooks held out his hand, and they shook. "Was it the races or Tattersall's? I remember there was horseflesh involved."

Raines gray eyes sparkled. "Tattersall's. I bought that magnificent white stepper."

"Ah, yes. How did he work out?"

"He's my favorite mount. Have any of you seen Charles?" asked the viscount. "He was supposed to meet me here."

"I'm afraid my cousin is always more than fashionably late, but he'll be here," assured Evelina. She waved over the guests as her parents came in from the garden. "Shall I introduce you to my father and mother?"

He squinted over the heads of the guests. His face went pale, and he made his excuses. "I would enjoy that very much at another time. I see an acquaintance I must speak to before they leave." He bowed and disappeared into the crowd, his blond head still visible as he moved away.

"Who was that?" asked Lady Franklin. "He seemed familiar."

"Lord Raines, a friend of Charles." Evie wondered at the man's odd reaction. What had alarmed him? *A cursed rum touch,* her grandfather would have said.

"Raines, did you say?" asked Sir Horace in a harsh tone.

Evie studied her father. He wore a frown and his jaw twitched. "Do you know him? Is he disreputable?"

"The man I knew certainly was. But the viscount I was acquainted with was much older. Has to be his son. The scoundrel must be dead, then. Good riddance."

"Horace, that's a terrible thing to say." Lady Franklin rapped him with her fan. "We're in mixed company."

"My apologies, ladies, but avoid that family. The apple

never falls far from the tree," he said with a warning scowl. "I need a drink."

This was a new side to her father. She'd never heard such malevolence in his voice. It piqued her interest. Another conversation with Lord Raines might be enlightening.

Near the end of the evening, the opportunity arose. She saw the viscount walk onto the terrace for some air and followed. Outside, it was still muggy but a slight breeze cooled her neck.

"Lord Raines, are you enjoying the dance?" she asked, leaning on the white rail that overlooked the garden. She inhaled the clinging scent of iris and sweet pea. The moon was nearly full, but clouds blocked out the stars. "You dashed away so quickly."

"Er, yes, I had to speak someone." He stood next to her, hands clasped behind his back. "How is your sister?"

"I think she's doing well. She's in Scotland with my grandmother for a visit." Evie pressed her lips together, wondering if she should ask. "Did you like her?"

"Of course, I..." He paused as he took in Evie's questioning expression. "Not-not, er, in that way."

"Oh, you dashed away so quickly before meeting my parents, and you got along with Fenella so well. I thought if you were interested in her—"

"Absolutely not!"

His words and adamant tone hung between them. "I didn't mean to offend you!" She turned on her heel, but he caught her elbow.

"Wait, please. I didn't mean to insult you or your sister." Remorse darkened his gray eyes. "Did you know my mother passed?"

Guilt squeezed her chest. "I'm so sorry. No, Charles didn't mention it."

"She had suffered for so long that it really was a blessing."

Evelina placed a hand on his arm. "It's hard to lose a loved one. Is there anything I can do?"

He shook his head and turned back to the garden, staring out into the darkness. "She told me a secret just before she died."

His voice was thick, and her heart went out to him. "A confession?"

He nodded. "What would you do if you found out that your entire life was based on a lie? The man you thought you were, was a sham?"

Evie swallowed. She hadn't expected some hidden family scandal to enter the conversation. "I don't know. I'd never thought about it. I'm sure, whatever it is, she did what she thought was best."

"She lied to me, and she lied to her husband. The man I thought was my father..." He laughed, a harsh sound that sent goosebumps up her arm. "He was unscrupulous in business and not a pleasant man, I'll admit. We didn't get along most of the time, but he was still my father..."

Sir Horace's reaction to the name made sense now, after Raines comment about the late viscount's reputation. Still, sons didn't always inherit a parent's traits.

"I think of the years I spent caring for her"—he ran a hand through his pale blond hair—"and my reward was a deathbed confession. But some sins can never be forgiven."

How did one respond to such a revelation? Was Lord Raines saying his mother had been unfaithful? Evelina was at a loss for words. She had no idea how to soothe his anguish.

"Did she tell you who your father was?"

He looked at her, horror in his eyes. He swiped his hand over his face. "I must apologize. I had a shock tonight, and I'm not myself tonight. I don't usually rattle on about my affairs."

"I'm glad to listen."

Raines turned to her. "Yes, that's why I came to London. I wanted to see him, meet him. Now that I'm here, I don't know. Perhaps it's better to leave the past in the past. What would it change?"

"Does he know he has a son?"

"A by-blow, you mean."

She sighed. This poor man, led to believe one thing all his life. It must be the like balancing on the crumbling foundation of a building, and one day, the entire structure gives way. "Will you contact him?"

He shook his head. "I doubt it, but I apologize again for burdening you with my woes. I've been brooding over this for weeks…"

"Sometimes it's easier to share your feelings with a stranger. I promise it will go no further." She touched his arm again, and he tensed. "I hope you come to terms with it and find your father."

Lord Raines pushed away from the railing and looked down at her. "If I believe some good may come of it, I would consider it. For now, I shall keep it to myself and return to my estate next week." He held out his elbow. "Thank you for being a friend and listening. Talking about it eased my soul a bit, I think. Time will be an ally and while I make a decision."

Evelina's fingers gripped his forearm, and he led her back into the crowded ballroom. She has the oddest feeling about this man. If only she could put her finger on it.

CHAPTER FOURTEEN

August 1819
London

Evelina stared at the calling card, her knuckles white as she gripped the silver tray. He was back in London. Finally, Lord Brecken was back. She fought the urge to squeal and jump up and down. Instead, she took the stairs two at a time and threw open her bedroom door.

"Louella," she called. "I must change. Hurry!"

She pulled off her white linen cap and grabbed her ivory comb, pulling it through her tresses. He would be back this afternoon, she was sure. It was their day at home, and he wouldn't wait to see her, would he?

By the time her maid entered the room, Evie was in a panic. What if he proposed today?

"What has you so befuddled, miss?" asked Louella.

"Lord Brecken is back in Town and left his card. I must be ready!"

"Well, why didn't you say so?" The maid marched to the wardrobe and found a sprigged muslin dress of pale Pomona green with tiny pink blossom embroidered along the hem and cuffs. The neckline was modest but didn't extend all the way to her neck. "Let's get you dressed, then we'll work on the hair."

As Louella finished weaving the ribbon through Evie's curls, they heard the clatter of hooves. "He's here, miss. Now hold still while I fasten your pendant."

Evie's heart raced. What if he'd had a change of heart? With trembling hands, she picked up her fan and looped it over her wrist. She took the steps slowly, breathing deep to calm her racing pulse. The butler met her at the bottom of the stairs.

"Lord Brecken has arrived and is in the study with your father. Sir Horace asked that you wait in the parlor."

She nodded and walked down the hall, her mind whirling with the conversation between her father and Lord Brecken. A hand went to her stomach to calm the butterflies battering to get out. She sat down on the chaise longue. Fragrant red and white roses were arranged in a vase on a low table. The parlor was bright and cheery with the windows open to take advantage of any breeze. Usually, they'd have been in the country by now, attending one party or another. Evie had turned down several invitations, afraid to miss the earl's return.

She sat with her hands clasped in her lap, her feet sweeping the Persian rug as her legs swung back and forth. Studying the delicate, hand-painted vines on the wall paper, she willed her breathing to slow.

Though she'd been waiting for him, Evie startled when the door opened. Lord Brecken entered and stopped in front of her.

"Miss Evelina," he rumbled.

"Lord Brecken." Evie couldn't breathe, couldn't move. It was the most important moment of her life.

"May I sit?" he asked, not waiting for an answer. Before she could turn fully to face him, her hand was in his. "Have you missed me?"

She nodded, afraid to trust her voice. Her throat was so thick, she could barely swallow. Tears threatened, and she blinked to hold them back.

"You were in my thoughts every day," he said. The sun caught the brilliant specks of green in his eyes. His dimple appeared when he smiled down at her, and her insides tumbled. "I've spoken with your father."

She held her breath. Oh, heavens. *Say it! Ask me! I can't stand another second*, she pleaded silently.

"The day I met you, my life changed. When I thought of marriage, I thought of a proper match and my duties as an earl. It was all part of my responsibilities when I inherited the title." He rubbed his thumb over the back of her hand, the warmth sending a shiver over her skin. "You made me realize that marriage can also mean a partnership, a bonding of two people who make life better for one another by... simply being together."

Her heart pounded. The blood rushing through her head made it hard to hear him, and she leaned forward so as not to miss a word, a syllable.

"I saw you skating on the Serpentine last February. Call it fate, call it destiny, but I was drawn to you. I realized when we met that my heart was half-empty. You made me whole, made me love you. Miss Evelina, will you do me the honor of becoming my wife?"

Her breath quickened, her chest rising and falling. A tear slipped down her cheek as she nodded, a watery smile curving her lips. "Yes," she whispered. "Yes, Madoc." Oh, how she loved to say his name.

Madoc leaned forward and pressed his lips to hers. His fingers brushed back her curls; his knuckles grazed her cheek. Her hands pushed against his hard chest, feeling the solid strength, and she closed her eyes. He loved her. He *loved* her.

Madoc pulled her close, his lips moving from her mouth to her jaw and down her neck. When he moaned, a giggle bubbled up her throat.

"You find this scene amusing?" he murmured against her earlobe, his breath ticklish.

She shook her head. "It's nerves. I've been so anxious for your return."

He cradled her face between his palms. "I never want you to worry about that again. Know that my feelings are steadfast and will never change." His thumb swiped her wet cheek. "And I only allow happy tears."

"They are," she assured him, leaning her face into his palm. "So very happy."

***

Two days later

"Miss Evelina, I'd like you to meet my mother, Lady Brecken."

Madoc watched the two women appraise one another. The younger with openness and optimism, the other, guarded and reserved. His mother had no illusions of marriage. She'd assured him that she only wanted to know Evelina would be a loyal and obedient wife.

"I've heard so much about you, Lady Brecken." Evelina gave a slight curtsy. "Would you care for some tea?" They sat on the chintz wingback chairs. A table in the center held a tea service and an arrangement of sweet-smelling flowers.

"That would be lovely, thank you." The countess sat, arranging her black bombazine skirt and tugging on the black lace gloves. "My son has told me of your family and background. Your mother must be quite pleased with the match."

"Mama!" His jaw clenched. They had agreed not to mention the Franklin's lesser status or the dowry. She should have been happy this wedding taking place at all, rather than acting high in the instep and insulting his betrothed.

"She's beside herself with joy," agreed Evelina, casting a reassuring glance at Madoc. "I realize a baronet's daughter is a step down for an earl, but love doesn't see titles."

"No, it doesn't. But love doesn't pay the taxes, or repair the tenants' roofs, or purchase livestock, does it?" Lady Brecken sipped her tea, setting the delicate china cup onto the saucer with a clatter. "But dowries do."

Madoc closed his eyes. His fingers curled into his palms as resisted the urge to throttle his mother. What was she doing? He was supposed to choose the time and the place to explain.

"Mama, don't—" Evelina's questioning gaze stopped his next words. "Let me explain."

"Your dowry is the answer to our prayers. It will restore the estate and my husband's name in the county." The countess smiled sweetly. "You really are a godsend, my dear."

"My dowry?" asked Evelina, her voice pitched high. She blinked at the countess and turned her gaze back to Madoc. "My dowry?"

"It doesn't affect my feelings for you—"

"You need my dowry?" Her bottom lip trembled.

"It's why he came to London. I was concerned what I might have to endure. Some of those mushrooms are so crude. But you, Miss Evelina, are a beauty. We are truly fortunate."

Madoc felt the floor tilt. "I'm marrying Evie because I love her." He moved next to his betrothed and took her hand. "It's not what you think."

She refused to meet his eyes, staring at their entwined hands. "Are you in need of funds?"

He sighed and glared at his mother. "Yes."

"Did you come to London to find a wealthy bride?" Evie spoke in a husky, monotone.

"Yes, but—"

She yanked her hand from his and stood. "It was a pleasure to meet you, Lady Brecken. I'm afraid I'm not feeling well, a bit of a megrim. I hope to see you another time." She curtsied and rushed from the room.

"What in the devil are you thinking?" he growled. "Do you know what you've done?"

"I do." His mother took a sip of tea and looked him in the eye. "I know my son. He would put off telling his fiancée about his need for a dowry. He would hem and haw, use the excuse he hadn't found the right time, the right place, the right words."

"So, you took it upon yourself to do it for me?" He paced the length of the room, trying to control the anger that slowly erupted.

"I did. It occurred to me that you have the chance for the kind of marriage I had, the second time. If you go into this marriage being dishonest, she'll resent you for it. It would be better to have a wife you don't care a whit for than to live with a woman you love who despises you. We are not the fragile creatures you think we are. It would hurt her more knowing you didn't trust her with the truth, than the fact you need her money."

Lady Brecken set the cup down and stood, laying a hand

on Madoc's arm. "Can you imagine the pain of seeing her every day for the rest of your life, but never having her love?"

Madoc stared at her, wondering how to repair this, knowing she was right.

"Now, inform the butler I would like to visit with Lady Franklin while you speak with your betrothed."

***

Evie sobbed into her pillow. He was a brute, a sop. A terrible, horrible lout. How could he do this to her? She had been sure he loved her. What a wet goose she was. When a knock sounded at her door, she yelled, "Go away!"

"Evie, my sweet, open the door," called Sir Horace from the other side. "I know you're upset, but I need to speak with you."

She sniffed and wiped her cheeks with her palms. "Come in."

Sir Horace entered and held out his arms. Evie rushed into his embrace, snuffling against his silk waistcoat. "He only wanted your money," she wailed.

"There, there, Evie. This is all my fault."

She pushed back from him. "Your fault?" Could this day get any worse?

Her father recounted the discussion he'd had with Lord Brecken at the club. He told her of the late earl, the bamboozling estate manager, Brecken's hesitancy to ask for her hand, and the agreement they had arrived at. "It was my idea not to tell you. He's a fine man, and he cares for you deeply. Believe me, I know a man in love when I see one."

"Would he marry me if I were poor?" she asked petulantly.

"The world isn't so simple, Evie. I can tell you if he didn't need the money, he would still marry you. You must show him some grace in this situation." Sir Horace held her by the shoulders. "You are a clever girl with good instincts. In your heart, you know what's true."

He kissed her forehead. "He's waiting for you in the garden whenever you're ready. You have my support whether you accept or reject his proposal."

Evie watched her father walk away, the earl's recent words revolving in her brain.

When I thought of marriage, I thought of a proper match and my duties as an earl. It was all part of my responsibilities when I inherited the title.

She sat down at the dressing table and scowled at her puffy eyes in the mirror. The day had been so promising. What was she to do now? She closed her eyes, and Madoc's face came to her. His eyes glistened with panic, a reflection of his love and concern.

Of course he loved her.

You made me realize that marriage can also mean a partnership, a bonding of two people who make life better for one another by... simply being together.

She took in a deep breath. And another. Then another.

Know that my feelings are steadfast and will never change.

. . .

Her father was right, she needed to trust her own instincts. Evie felt his love in each shared glance, each smile, each touch. She should be thanking fate rather than cursing it.

After washing her face and adjusting her dress, Evie rushed down the stairs and out to the garden. "Madoc," she called, pausing at the trellis and barely noticing the heavy scent of wisteria.

"Evelina." He stood next to the fountain, hands clasped behind his back, his face ravaged. Her heart ached for him. He'd been through so much in the past months. She could be the balm to heal the wounds of the past.

Evie picked up her skirts and ran down the path, throwing herself against his chest. "Tell me you love me," she panted as she hugged him with all her might. "Tell me."

He scooped her into his arms and sat down on a stone bench. "I love you, Evelina Franklin. I need you like I need my first breath in the morning. You are the day to my night, the stars to my moon." He peppered her face with kisses.

"Promise me you'll say it every day and never forget." Life without this man would be hollow. It didn't matter what led him to her. Their fates were entwined.

"I swear." He kissed her mouth, hard and demanding, and she wiggled in his lap.

"Should we join your mother?" she asked in his ear, biting the soft lobe.

"Lady Franklin is keeping her company." Madoc kissed her eyes, then her nose. "It seems my mother feared I wouldn't tell you before the wedding. She said it would be a wedge between us that could never be removed."

"My father told me of his part too. I understand now."

"You must also promise me something." He tipped her chin, his hazel eyes serious.

"Name it." She would do anything for this man.

"You make me whole. I was half a man these last two months." He brushed her lips. "Never, ever doubt that *you* are enough for me. I would have found a way for you to be mine, with or without a dowry."

"I promise to never doubt your love," Evie whimpered as his mouth closed over hers and passion claimed all thought. As soon as the world stopped spinning, they'd plan their future. Together.

CHAPTER FIFTEEN

September 1819

"How much is left?" Madoc wondered what would give him more satisfaction, retrieving some of his lost inheritance or killing Caerton. Perhaps he could have both.

"Three-quarters, I'm guessing," answered Walters. "He's half-flash and half-foolish, so full of himself yet so easily gulled."

Madoc did a quick mental count. They'd found the solicitor who'd collaborated with Caerton. Walters had uncovered the evidence in his office, including receipts with dates and names. The accountant had tried to feign ignorance, that he didn't know the items he'd sold "on the side" had been stolen. His business was now closed, and he sat in a crowded cell awaiting trial. The swindler wouldn't hang or rot in Fleet Prison. Either was fine with the earl.

Fifteen thousand pounds recovered. It was a start.

Rather than the constable arresting Caerton, Madoc and Walters had devised a more satisfying plan. After all the suffering the bloody thief had put his family and tenants through, Niall would realize some of the agony he'd caused.

"My *acquaintances* have been gambling with him the entire summer. They win some, lose some, and the cull doesn't suspect a thing." Walters rubbed his hands together. They'd collected three thousand pounds so far from the winnings. "The boys claim a hundred pounds per thousand, as agreed upon. They've put a lot of time into this investigation. Tonight, we finish off the blethering oaf."

Niall Caerton hadn't trusted a bank to keep his money. Walters had searched his room and found a heavy pouch of coin but no bank notes. The bulk of the fortune was hidden somewhere.

"He's in a decent neighborhood in Covent Garden. When we meet tonight, he believes Smythe and I are bringing him to a private club. Which we are, in a sense." Walters grinned. "This will be a sweet end, my lord."

Walters would be introduced as a man of influence who was bringing them to an exclusive gaming hell. The foursome would arrive at the back entrance of a rented shop and escorted to the "private rooms" upstairs, now transformed into a small gaming den. He himself would tend the dice for the hazard table, while Brooks oversaw the card game of Vingt-et-un. Other associates of Walters would be random customers.

Madoc waited in full guise, though he didn't know if Niall Caerton would recognize him after so many years. When the group entered, he ground his teeth. The peep-o-day boy hadn't changed. Same pale face and sly blue eyes, sandy hair, weak chin, and lewd smile. His small eyes darted about the room hungrily and glanced off Madoc quickly. Walters led him to the Vingt-et-un table. It had begun.

Over the next hour, Caerton won some and lost some. By midnight, sweat dotted his brow, and he wiped at the freckles on his cheeks with a handkerchief. Madoc knew many men addicted to gambling, and this Welshman was no different. The gleam in his eyes, the fervor of the next win would lead them to his hiding place.

"Sir, you're out of credit. I'm afraid we'll need another bank note to place another bet." Brooks played the dealer perfectly. Madoc bit his lip to keep the smile from his face.

"I don't have any more with me," said Caerton. "I'm good for my debt."

"I'm sure you are, sir, but we do not accept credit here." Brooks' brown eyes even appeared apologetic. Blast, but he owed his friend.

"I can get more," pleaded Caerton. "I'll return within the hour."

"As you wish, sir," agreed Brooks, his smile wide.

Caerton left the building, and activity stopped. "I'll go first," said Madoc, peeling off his gray wig and spectacles. "Follow me in case the plan goes awry."

It didn't. Niall went to an old church on the outskirts of Covent Garden. He strode into the cemetery and stopped at a headstone. Pushing it backwards, he reached beneath it and retrieved a box. He opened it, pulled something out, and tucked it in his coat. When he reached the cemetery gate, Madoc stepped out.

"Hello, Niall."

"Wh-who are you?" Caerton asked, a hand going to his chest where he'd placed the bank note.

"Lord Brecken," he responded with a tight smile. "Don't you recognize me?"

"He's dead. Out of my way, I have business to attend to." Niall tried to walk past but Madoc grabbed him by the collar.

"What are you doing? I'm a man of means. Unhand me."

"I was a man of means until you embezzled my inheritance," he snarled.

Caerton paled. "L-lord M-madoc?"

"You do recognize me."

"How did you find me?" he whispered.

"I'm as tenacious as my father."

Caerton's eyes were wide. He held out a hand, backed up several steps, then turned and ran. Madoc followed and tackled him. When Caerton swung and connected with Madoc's jaw, the earl lost control. It all came back to him— the lost years with his father, the crumbling estate, the hopelessness in the tenants' eyes, his mother's tears.

He sat up and drove one fist, then the other into Caerton's face, pounding him again and again until another pair of hands gripped his shoulders and pulled him back.

"Ye won't get the justice you're looking for by killing him now, my lord." Walters' voice or reason sounded dimly in his ears as he panted. "We have a plan, remember?"

Madoc nodded. "Yes. Yes, we have plan." He caught his breath and rubbed his knuckles. "I'm fine now, Walters. Thank you."

"What plan?" whimpered Caerton.

"You're taking a trip," said Walters, "back to Wales. You've missed your village, haven't ye?"

Niall shook his head, his eyes wide with fear and his lip trembling. "I can't go back there. They'll—"

"What? Kill you?" Madoc asked, a wicked curving his lips. "No, you're safe enough. I've instructed the new estate manager to hold you while you await a trial. It may take several months for that, though. You know how few magistrates there are in Wales."

"But we have no jail in Brecknock."

Madoc laughed, a hollow sound. "We've made arrangements. A new barn has been built for the livestock. There are plenty of empty sheds for you to sleep in at night, and many tenants willing to put you up in theirs. Your daylight hours will be spent in the same place, though."

Walters yanked the man from the ground and pulled his hands behind his back, tying his wrists. "Don't ye want to know where you'll be?"

"We've found the old pillory, and you'll be on display for the villagers every day until you are sentenced. They won't kill you, but..." He chuckled. "They'll make you suffer as they did, with words and deeds."

Madoc envisioned Caerton with his hands and head enclosed in the wooden block, subjected to taunts and whatever dirt, dung, or refuse the tenants threw at him. Brecknock would have their revenge before the courts.

"No, no, I can't go back there. I'll never get a trial. I'll—"

"Enough!" yelled Madoc. "Your fate has been decided."

***

One week later

Exquisite. Evelina stood before the mirror while the modiste fussed and clucked with pins held between her teeth. Mid-morning rays slanted through the open sash, cooling the room. A light breeze billowed the sheer cambric curtains across the arched windows. As Evie fidgeted, clingy white satin shimmered beneath a champagne overdress of Brussels point lace that added a glow to her skin. Gold embroidery trimmed the cap sleeves and hem, as well as the satin and lace train. Gold silk gloves and slippers finished the ensemble.

"You will be the most beautiful bride," Fenella said, blinking back tears. "What accessories will you wear?"

"Brecken's mother gave me a tiara of thin twisted gold and clusters of pearls. It looks like white roses entwined in golden vines." Evie's voice was wistful. "She wore it at her wedding."

"So, the two of you get along well?" she asked.

"Of course they do," interrupted Lady Franklin. "Who would not appreciate Evelina's delicate beauty and flawless manners?"

"We've come to an understanding," Evie said quietly. "She's not pleased the ceremony will take place in London rather than their family home in Wales."

"No one would travel so far to a Welsh estate. He spends most of his time in London anyway," huffed their mother.

"Mama, could you give Fenella and me some time alone? It's been so long since we've seen each other." She gave Lady Franklin a sweet smile. "Please, Mama?"

"Well, I suppose." Their mother moved to the door and paused. "I want to see the final fitting before Madame leaves."

She waited until Lady Franklin closed the door. Evie had been so relieved when her sister had written to her about Lachlan MacNaughton, a Scot she'd lost her heart to. Her only concern for Fenella was their mother's reaction. If she and Papa put their heads together, Evie was sure their mother would come round.

"How will you tell Mama about Lachlan?" she asked.

"That is not why you had her leave the room. I see the fear in your eyes," said Fenella with a wag of her finger. "Tell me what's bothering you."

. . .

159

"I'm having doubts," Evie whispered. "While Brecken's been successful with investments since gaining the title, he cannot afford to revive the estate without..."

"Your dowry. Do you fear the money persuaded him into marriage more than you?"

Evie nodded and sniffed, her eyes glistening. "He speaks of love, and I do believe him, but there's this nasty little voice in the back of my head that taunts me."

"The Lord Brecken I first met was enamored of you at first sight. He had no idea of your dowry." She laid a hand on her sister's cheek. "I can only imagine your time together enhancing his attraction."

"The reason he was attending the season was to find an heiress." Evie blinked. "His mother was pressuring him."

"We certainly understand overbearing mothers."

The modiste snorted.

"Dear sister, when you enter the room, his eyes see nothing else. It's love in his gaze. I'm sure of it." She hugged Evie.

"Do you really think so?" She bit her lip, wanting to be convinced.

Fenella nodded and hugged her sister. "I swear it."

Evie wiped at the corner of her eyes. "Thank you, dear Fenella. I'm so glad you've come."

"By the way, you hadn't mentioned moving to Wales in your letters."

"Nothing has been decided as of yet, so there was no need to." She made a circle as Madame pulled at her skirt. "He said we will make all decisions together."

"See? He's not only handsome but reasonable."

Evie pulled up her curls and turned as the modiste sat back on her heels.

"Puhfecshun," the modiste said around the pins in her mouth.

. . .

***

Rain splattered against the roof as they settled against the squabs of the carriage. "This means good luck!" exclaimed Sir Horace.

"Why do people say that?" asked Evelina. She couldn't imagine a drenched bride being lucky.

"It's about knots. Handfasting included knots tied around the wrists of the couple. When a knot is wet, it's twice as hard to untangle. So it's believed your marriage will be twice as strong." Fenella grinned at her mother's frown at the mention of a Scottish custom.

Evie's stomach was a bumblebath. It was her wedding day. Miss Evelina Franklin would walk into the St. George's Hanover Square Church, and Lady Brecken would walk out. She gripped Fenella's hand as the carriage halted and a footman opened the door. Sir Horace exited first and then assisted Evie, his wife and oldest daughter.

"Are you nervous, my sweet?" asked her father as they made their way up the steps.

"My stomach has finally calmed. The mint tea Mama prepared helped."

They entered the church and her breath hitched as she took in the stunning interior. A typical Anglican church, it had a spacious nave and tall, box pews facing the aisle. Galleries and a balcony overlooked the nave on three sides. The dark intricately carved wood and ornate plastered arched ceilings contrasted with the brilliant stained-glass windows behind the altar.

Her mother and sister took their places, and then her father escorted her to Lord Brecken. She swallowed, wondering if his hands were trembling as badly as hers.

In front of her stood Lord Brecken in black tails, satin

breeches, and a coffee-brown waistcoat, embroidered with gold to match the trim of Evie's dress. An intricate white cravat was perfectly tied with a diamond pin set in the middle. His dark hair was combed back, his beard neatly trimmed, and his smile genuine as he gazed down at his new bride. The love in his hazel eyes eased the tension in her shoulders, and she let out a sigh.

As the ceremony began and the vicar opened his bible, Madoc leaned over and whispered in her ear, "I'll explain later, but I no longer require your dowry. I wanted you to know."

Her eyes flew to his handsome face, wide and questioning, and he winked in response. He didn't need the money? What had happened in the past week? Madoc had left London in the middle of the night and returned only yesterday. She hadn't seen him. In fact, she'd had a nightmare that he jilted her.

Evie clutched her nosegay, unable to wipe the smile from her face. Matrimony was a serious endeavor, and here she stood with a ridiculous grin on her face. Oh, how she loved this man. Destiny may have used her dowry to entwine their paths, but it was their love that held them close.

The vicar peered out at the guests. "Therefore, if any man can show any just cause, why they may not lawfully be joined together, let him now speak, or else hereafter forever hold his peace."

Their vows were said in a blur, Evie lost in the moment and the joy of marrying the man she loved.

Madoc took her hand in his and spoke his vows. "With this ring, I thee wed, with my body I thee worship, and with all *my* worldly goods, I thee endow." He slipped the simple gold band onto her finger, and they both knelt before the vicar, who continued with another prayer.

The vicar joined their right hands and said loudly, "Those

whom God hath joined together let no man put asunder."

After the wedding, the parish registry was signed. As the group filed out of the small office, Madoc held her back.

"I'm sorry if I took you by surprise at the beginning of the ceremony, but I wanted you to know before you said your vows. I love *you*, Lady Brecken, with all my heart." He pulled her in his arms and brushed her lips.

She raised a palm to his face, parting her lips for him. The wings fluttered in her belly, and thoughts of their wedding night her heart pound. His mouth claimed hers, velvet against silk, and desire sent heat swooshing to her core Tonight she would know him as a woman knows a man.

"I thank fate and the grace of God the day I saw you skating on the Serpentine. You stole my heart, Evie. I humbly give you mine in return." He kissed her again, a slow, sensual dance against her lips.

Their entire lives were before them. She would be mistress of her own castle, a dozen children if she had her way, and a man who adored her. Evie would wake up to his devastatingly handsome face every morning and see the love in his hazel eyes each night before she closed her own.

She blinked back the tears. *Not even happy tears*, he had told her once. Pish and petunias, a bride could cry on her own wedding day, couldn't she?

Reviews are the lifeblood of authors. If you've enjoyed this story, please consider leaving a few words at your favorite retailer.

Keep updated on future releases, exclusive excerpts, and prizes by following my newsletter:

https://www.subscribepage.com/k3f1z5

. . .

If you liked to read the Earl of Darby's story, find it here!

If you'd like to read Fenella's story, find it here! The MacNaughton Castle romances is my steamy series.

SNEAK PEEK: EARL OF KEYWORTH

EARL OF KEYWORTH
Wicked Earls' Club
Seductive Scoundrels
By
COLLETTE CAMERON®

PROLOGUE

My darling, not a day goes by that I do not wish we were together.
  I should have defied Keyworth.
  I should have been brave and strong
  and escaped when I knew I carried you, my precious love.
  But Landry needed me.
  I was so frightened for him...
  Can you ever forgive me?

~Letter from the Countess of Keyworth to her daughter, Lenora.
  Never sent. Ripped up and burned.

Faringcroft Park—Earl of Keyworth's Country Seat

Lancaster, England
16 February 1810—Late Evening

Sweat beaded his brow as Landry Audsley, Earl of Keyworth, held his dying mother's cold, frail hand. A roaring fire hissed and snapped angrily in the hearth. Regardless, the Countess of Keyworth shivered, her feeble form racked by chills.

The suffocating heat fairly choked him, making it impossible to breathe. Or perhaps it was the unshed tears constricting his throat and cramping his lungs that made the simple task of drawing air into his lungs difficult.

He tenderly drew another blanket from the foot of the bed over his mother's emaciated form.

Always slight of build, his once pretty-as-a-pansy mother had wasted away these past months until only a shell of the woman he adored remained. She was only two-and-forty— much, *much* too young to die.

"I love you, Landry," she said, reaching out to graze his cheek.

A sob caught in Landry's throat and, with grim resolve, he quashed the evidence of his heartbreak.

"I love you too, Mama."

He nearly strangled on the five short words. There was so much more he wanted to say.

His mother was all that was gentle and sweet, compassionate and kind. The opposite of the coldhearted, mercenary blighter she had entered into an arranged marriage with. The previous earl had preceded her in death only last year, and within months she had also fallen ill.

So bloody, bloody damned unfair.

Providence. Destiny. Fate. Whatever higher force had dealt this unjust hand was capricious and immensely cruel.

Scorching tears stung Landry's eyes.

His mother's delicate features, ashen in contrast to the

pale lavender pillows she rested upon, blurred before his gaze. Summoning gritty determination, he blinked the stinging moisture away, lest Mama witness his grief and become even more distraught.

This dear woman's unconditional love was what had kept him from becoming a replica of the former earl: harsh, unforgiving, selfish, and an abusive, sodding cockscum.

Some claimed giving one's life for another was the greatest gift, and Landry supposed it was. But loving someone unconditionally, even when it guaranteed you'd suffer at another's hands because of that love...

Well, that made his mother a bloody saint in his mind.

Landry had not shed a tear or felt the minutest flicker of grief when his father had kicked off his mortal coil in a most befitting manner—an apoplexy while shagging a Covent Garden doxy.

In truth, it was a wonder the previous earl had not perished from the clap or pox decades ago. It was no more than he deserved.

However, the inflexible, unrelenting reality of never seeing his beloved mother again nearly eviscerated Landry.

God, he screamed silently. Desperately.

"Landry, I must...tell you something," Mama whispered, her voice the merest whisper of sound. An old woman's weak, quavery voice. Not his mother's dulcet tones.

"Shh, Mama," he soothed, leaning down to press his mouth to her too-cool, pale-as-milk forehead. "Save your strength."

It would not be long now.

He swallowed the grief strangling him.

Soon his sweet mother would draw her last labored breath.

Doctor Rendle had left an hour ago. Shaking his silvery-white head, he'd patted Landry's shoulder in a fatherly fashion. "I am deeply sorry, my lord. There is nothing more to be done. The countess will pass shortly. I have given her laudanum to keep her comfortable."

Rage burgeoned in Landry's chest at the unfairness.

By God in heaven.

Evil people should die young.

Those as decent and loving as his mother should live to a ripe old age. To see their son married and to hold their grandchildren in their loving embrace. To enjoy the peace and happiness that was denied them for far, *far* too long.

The muffled weeping of Warner, his mother's lady's maid for the past two decades, came from the corner she huddled in miserably. The sniffling and watery shudders agitated Landry, but he did not have the heart to order her to leave the bedchamber.

He well knew how much Warner loved his mother. How, she too, had willingly acted as a buffer between the dying countess and the previous earl's violent rages and calculated cruelty.

"No, Landry. You *must*…listen to me." Mama grasped his waistcoat, weakly urging him nearer. "I should have told you long ago. Certainly after Keyworth died."

Landry had removed his cravat and coat before the doctor left. It somehow seemed wrong to be attired in starchy formality at a time like this. Besides, the bedchamber was a blistering inferno, the scarlet and orange flames in the hearth fiercely battling each other for dominance in a skirmish neither would win.

Sweat trickled down his back and soaked his underarms. *His* discomfort did not matter. He'd endure hell's fires if it meant easing Mama's suffering a single jot.

Landry forced a smile, though his facial muscles protested the effort, and a merciless vice crushed his ribs, threatening to pulverize them into dust.

"What is it?" he asked, wishing she would save her strength. Each additional minute with her was a treasure he could store up in his heart and memory.

"You have a sister," she whispered through blue-tinted lips.

A sister?

What?

"What?" Landry drew back, his befuddled mind trying to comprehend what she had murmured.

Was she delusional?

Hallucinating?

Was that a sign of impending death?

Pressing two fingers to his temple, he searched the recesses of his mind.

Had Dr. Rendle mentioned anything of that nature?

Landry honestly did not know.

He could not remember half of what the kindly doctor had told him.

Grief had turned Landry's mind into a foggy, cottony, befuddled mess.

"I named her Lenora, Landry," Mama sobbed softly, a sodden handkerchief pressed to her mouth. "Keyworth was *not* her father."

So his gentle-hearted mother had taken a lover.

Brava for her.

She certainly deserved a sliver of happiness after having been married to the monster she had called husband for four-and-twenty years. Regardless, his sire's hypocrisy was beyond maddening and equally infuriating.

Where was this sister?

Shunted off to live in obscurity with a distant relative?

Squeezing her hand, he said, "It is all right, Mama."

For what else did one say to one's dying parent when they were confessing their darkest secret?

"He...he did not even permit me to hold her," she muttered raggedly, almost as if speaking to herself. Repeating a phrase she had no doubt murmured over and over and over again to herself in her sorrow.

"She would be ten years old now, my little girl," Mama said.

Scorching wrath tunneled through Landry's veins in the next heartbeat. He struggled to keep the anger from showing on his face or manifesting in his voice.

He knew of three boys born on the wrong side of the blanket his father had sired—all by different women. And all of whom had been servants in the debaucher's employ.

Undoubtedly, more of his seed had found fertile soil in the countless other women from the filthiest slatterns to the nobles' perfumed and powdered wives he'd swived. Worse than a rutting bull, the previous earl had not been the least selective or discreet in whom he tupped.

In his typical callous fashion, the reprobate had dismissed his pregnant servants on the grounds of promiscuousness. Likely as not, the cockscum had forced himself on them.

When Landry became the earl, he had hired Dirby Madagan, a detective, to locate each ill-used woman and had settled a generous portion on those women and their sons.

It was the least he could do.

And yet...it still was not nearly enough for the disgrace and humiliation the poor misused women had endured. Would continue to endure, for the status of illegitimacy would forever hang over his half-brothers' heads.

He had seen to it that the boys received an education, and when they were of an age, he would help them in the vocation of their choice.

How it must've enraged his father to have sired three more sons that he could never claim, while his wife had never born him another child. Just the one heir. Landry. No spare to satisfy the old earl's ego or guarantee the continuance of his spindly, unworthy branch of the family.

Reeling from his mother's confession, Landry asked, "Who is her father?"

All this time, he'd had a sister thirteen years younger than he.

Did she have quicksilver gray eyes and chestnut hair with reddish-bronze ribbons like their mother and him?

Did she possess the same sweet disposition and innocent beauty as their mother?

With apparent effort, his mother tipped her mouth upward a fraction.

"It does not matter, darling. He was not a nobleman or even landed gentry. He died…some time ago. Your father—"

Landry's mother winced, an expression of indescribable anguish flickering across her ravaged features. She licked her chapped lips. "He…"

"Yes?" Landry prompted. "He…?"

"Keyworth…killed him when he learned I was…with child."

"A *duel*?" Landry asked incredulously, unable to disguise his astonishment. His father had never seemed the honorable or courageous sort.

"No. Keyworth…he shot him in the back." A single crystalline tear trailed from the corner of one eye. "Keyworth gloated about it to me."

She had never called the late earl anything but Keyworth in a carefully neutral tone. As if she had retreated to someplace within herself where he could not hurt her anymore. As if inflicting any emotion into the word validated him in some manner.

"He delighted in telling me…all of the horrific details," she whispered brokenly. "How much my darling suffered."

The bloody, bloody murdering blackguard.

"I welcome death." A soft, faraway look entered her gray eyes. "I shall see my beloved again, at last."

"Do you have any idea where the earl would've sent the babe?" he asked, now desperate to gather as many details as he could so he could find Lenora.

Where did Landry start looking, for God's sake?

Ten years was a very long time—*too long?*— to attempt to find a trail likely gone arctic cold. Nonetheless, he must try.

Mama gave a shallow nod.

"Warner spied on Keyworth for me. He sent Lenora to live with a family in France. In the *Touraine* region. All of these years, I have tried to find her, but Lenora seemingly disappeared without a trace."

Her voice cracked, and the torment on her frail face ripped his heart from his chest. Another tear leaked from the corner of her eye.

That devil's spawn had sent an innocent babe to live in France while England and France had been at war? He'd probably hoped the child would die.

Or...had *he* disposed of the innocent babe?

Jesus.

That possibility soured Landry's stomach. Bile burned the back of his throat, and acrid bitterness flooded his mouth.

He abhorred the notion—couldn't conceive such evilness.

Regardless of how repulsive the thought, he must consider the possibility. If his sire could cold-bloodedly shoot a man in the back and take a babe at birth, he could also dispose of a defenseless infant without a qualm.

"The physician said I would bear no more children after Lenora. I laughed in Keyworth's face and told him I would cuckold him with any willing man hereafter." Mama coughed, her thin shoulders quaking.

Landry offered her a drink of water. After a small sip, his mother curved her mouth into a sardonic smile he'd never before seen upon her face. "It drove him positively mad, trying to figure out who I had been with. There wasn't anyone, of course. Not after...." Her lower lip quivered. "But I so despised him, I made it appear as if there were dozens and dozens."

"Heav'n has no rage, like love to hatred turned, nor hell fury, like a woman scorned."

A rather infamous line from playwright William Congreve whispered across Landry's mind.

How greatly he had underestimated his mother's strength and determination.

She focused her failing gaze across the room. "It was not hard to do, you know. Keyworth always wanted to believe the worst of me."

Aye, that festering sod's perception of everyone and everything was tinged with his pessimism and his own depraved outlook.

Mama clutched at Landry's hand, suddenly frantic. "Find her for me, Landry. She should be...with her brother."

She gasped, struggling to breathe for a pair of heartbeats.

A rusty blade skewering his heart would hurt less than watching her suffer—watching her die.

"Promise...me...my son," she rasped, her breathing ever more labored. "Before all else, please make finding your sister your priority." She drew in a shallow, rattling breath. "Then I can...rest in peace, knowing my children have each other."

Holding both of her hands in his, choking on the bevy of sobs throttling up his throat, Landry nodded. His tears flowed freely now, and he did not give a blacksmith's oath. The person he adored the most, his constant in an uncertain and often cruel world, was leaving him.

Forever.

At three-and-twenty, he would be alone.

He had no one.

Except for a ten-year-old sister *somewhere*.

And the possibility of a wife and children someday.

For his own sake, because of what his mother had longed for and been denied, and to spite the rotter burning in hell who'd sired him, Landry would not have a cold, distant marriage filled with icy disdain or fulminating anger.

By God, I would marry a flower hawker or a seamstress if she loved me, and I loved her.

"I shall find her, Mama." He pressed his lips to her icy knuckles.

"Thank you," she uttered so softly the sound barely slipped past her dry lips.

"I vow it," he swore. "I shall make finding Lenora my top priority."

She was gone before he finished his oath.

Connect with Collette!

www.collettecameron.com

Collette's Chèris VIP Reader Group

Newsletter (Get a FREE book!)

ABOUT THE AUTHOR

About Aubrey Wynne

Bestselling and award-winning author Aubrey Wynne is an elementary teacher by trade, champion of children and animals by conscience, and author by night. She resides in the Midwest with her husband, dogs, horses, mule, and barn cats. Obsessions include wine, history, travel, trail riding, and all things Christmas. Her Chicago Christmas series has received the Golden Quill, Aspen Gold, Heart of Excellence, and the Gayle Wilson Award of Excellence and twice nominated as a Rone finalist by InD'tale Magazine.

Aubrey's first love is medieval romance but after dipping her toe in the Regency period in 2018 with the *Wicked Earls' Club,* she was smitten. This inspired her spin-off series *Once Upon a Widow.* In 2020, she launched the Scottish Regency series *A MacNaughton Castle Romance* with Dragonblade Novels.

Social Media Links:
Website:
http://www.aubreywynne.com
Bookbub page:
https://www.bookbub.com/profile/aubrey-wynne
Sign up for my newsletter and don't miss future releases
https://www.subscribepage.com/k3f1z5

More Historical Romance

Once Upon a Widow series

Earl of Sunderland #1

Maggie award, International Digital Awards finalist

Grace Beaumont has seen what love can do to a woman. Her mother sacrificed her life to produce the coveted son and heir. A devastated father and newborn brother force her to take on the role of Lady Boldon at the age of fifteen. But Grace finds solace in the freedom and power of her new status.

Christopher Roker made a name for himself in the military. The rigor and pragmatism of the army suits him. When a tragic accident heaves Kit into a role he never wanted or expected, his world collides with another type of duty. Returning to England and his newfound responsibilities, the Wicked Earls' Club becomes a refuge from the glitter and malice of London society but cannot ease his emptiness.

Needing an escape from his late brother's memory and reputation, Kit visits the family estate for the summer. Lady Grace, a beauty visiting from a neighboring estate, becomes a welcome distraction. When the chance to return to the military becomes a valid possibility, the earl finds himself wavering between his old life and the lure of an exceptional—and unwilling—woman.

A Wicked Earl's Widow #2

Recommended by InD'tale Magazine

Eliza is forced into marriage with no idea her life will change for the better. Married less than a year, her unwilling rake of a husband is surprisingly kind to her—until his sudden death. The widowed Countess of Sunderland remains under her in-laws' protection to raise her newborn daughter. But her abusive father is on the brink of financial ruin and has plans for another wedding.

Nathaniel, Viscount of Pendleton, gains his title at the age of twelve. His kindly but shrewd estate manager becomes father and mentor, instilling in the boy an astute sense of responsibility and compassion for his tenants. Fifteen years later, his family urges him to visit London and seek a wife. The ideal doesn't appeal to him, but his sense of duty tells him it is the next logical step.

Lord Pendleton stumbles upon Eliza on the road, defending an elderly woman against ruffians. After rescuing the exquisite damsel in distress, he finds himself smitten. But Nate soon realizes he must discover the dark secrets of her past to truly save the woman he loves.

Rhapsody and Rebellion #3

Maggie finalist, nominated for Rone Award, InD'tale Magazine

A Scottish legacy... A political rebellion... Two hearts destined to meet...

Raised in his father's image, the Earl of Stanfeld is practical and disciplined. There are no gray lines interrupting the Gideon's black and white world. Until his mother has a dream and begs to return to her Highland home.

Alisabeth was betrothed from the cradle. At seventeen, she marries her best friend and finds happiness if not passion. In less than a year, a political rebellion makes her a widow. The handsome English earl arrives a month later and rouses her desire and a terrible guilt.

Crossing the border into Scotland, Gideon finds his predictable world turned upside down. Folklore, legend, and political unrest intertwine with an unexpected attraction to a feisty Highland beauty. When the earl learns of an English plot to stir the Scots into rebellion, he must choose his country or save the clan and the woman who stirs his soul.

Earl of Darby #4

**Holt Medallion Winner, NTRWA Reader's Choice Award, Nominated

for Rone Award, InD'tale magazine**

Miss Hannah Pendleton is nursing her pride after her childhood crush falls in love with another. Determined to break a few hearts of her own, she hurls herself into the exciting and hectic schedule of a first season. Always clever and direct, the smooth manners and practiced words of the gallant but meticulous bachelors do nothing to stir her soul until...

Since his wife's suicide on their wedding night, the Earl of Darby has carefully cultivated his rakish reputation. It keeps overprotective mamas at bay and provides him with unlimited clandestine affairs. But when Nicholas sees a lovely newcomer being courted by the devil himself, her innocence and candor revive the chivalry buried deep in his soul. The ice around Nicholas's heart cracks as he desperately tries to save Hannah and right a hideous wrong committed so long ago.

Earl of Brecken #5

A seductive Welsh earl on the brink of ruin. A wealthy cit in search of a hero.

Miss Evelina Franklin reads too many romance novels. She's certain a handsome duke—or dashing highwayman—is in her future. In the meantime, Evie entertains herself with the admirers vying for her fortune.

The Earl of Brecken needs cash. His late father left their Welsh estate in ruin, and his mother will not let him rest until it is restored to its former glory. Notorious for his seductive charm, he searches the ballrooms for a wealthy heiress. His choices are dismal until he meets Miss Franklin. Guileless and gorgeous with an enormous dowry, she seems the answer to his prayers. Until his conscience makes an unexpected appearance.

A MacNaughton Castle Romance series

Highland Regencies

"Witty and sensual!"

Verified Purchase Review

"Lovely characters and complicated family conflicts. You will easily get caught up in their lives."

Goodreads Review

A Merry MacNaughton Mishap (Prequel)

Rone finalist, InD'tale Magazine, N.N. Light Book Heaven finalist

Two feuding clans, one accidental encounter, a wee bit of holiday enchantment…

Peigi Craigg has tended to her family without complaint since her mother's death. But now they ask too much. The English landlord has offered her uncle, the Craigg chieftain, an escape from debt and starvation. The price: Peigi must become the earl's mistress. If she refuses, the remainder of their clan must leave the Highlands. If she agrees, her hope of a husband and family of her own are lost.

Calum MacNaughton rescues a man from an icy drowning, only to find he's a member of the rival Craigg clan. The man swears to repay Calum for saving his life and broaches the possibility of peace between the clans. Months later, the Craigg reappears with his most precious possession, hoping to settle his debt before the new year.

Now Calum has until Twelfth Night to convince her to stay.

Deception and Desire #1

Nominated for Rone award, InD'tale Magazine, N.N. Light Book Heaven award winner

Two rebellious souls… An innocent deception… One scorching catastrophe…

Fenella Franklin is too tall, too intelligent, and has no title. Her talents lie in numbers and a keen business mind, not in the art of flirtation. When she becomes the object of a cruel wager during her come-out in London, she vows to put off the penniless noblemen vying for her sizeable dowry. But her season is cut short after her mother discovers the subterfuge, and Fenella retreats to Scotland.

Lachlan MacNaughton has neither the temperament nor the patience to be the next MacNaughton chief, preferring to knock heads together rather than placate bickering clansmen. He readily accepts a reprieve to help with the family's textile mill in Glasgow. A sizzling chance encounter in the rain introduces him to the new *female* bookkeeper. His grandfather may want him back in the Highlands, but his heart has been lost in the Lowlands.

The attraction between Fenella and Lachlan sparks a passion not even two rebellious souls can deny. But an innocent deception tests their newfound love and threatens the freedom they both crave.

Allusive Love #2

A woman in love... An infuriating Scot... A tantalizing chase.

Kirstine MacDunn has loved Brodie MacNaughton forever. He returns her affection—as his best friend and confidante. After enduring one too many of his infatuations, she finally takes matters into her own hands.

Brodie knows it is his destiny to lead Clan MacNaughton, but his grandfather insists the honor goes to the oldest. When Brodie and his brothers struggle to convince the chief that tradition is not always the best path, he turns to Kirsty for support. She surprises him with more than advice. A kiss that sends unexpected fire through his veins.

Pride, Highland politics, and tragedy collide, proving Brodie's ability to lead. But when a resentful clan member's revenge threatens Kirsty, he realizes how precious and allusive true love can be.

The Count's Castaway

The Count's Castaway is a bit of swashbuckling adventure rolled into a romance. A brave heroine, a suave wanderlust hero, a ship on the high seas and unexpected love all blend together to make this a must-read.

N.N. Light's Book Heaven

He's escaping his past... She's running toward her future... The present just got interesting.

Torn from her bed and indentured to an American as a child, Katherine Wilken demands her freedom seven years later. Denied her liberty, she stows away on The Escape, hoping to return to England. But when the ship sets sail, so does her heart. Katie soon realizes she's once again a captive—of love.

Narrow escapes seem to be Count Alexandre Lecroix's lot in life. Fleeing France as a boy during the Reign of Terror, he's a man with no country and soon takes to the sea in search of his destiny. The Napoleonic Wars have filled his pockets and his zeal for excitement, but his heart remains hollow. When he discovers a feisty stowaway on board, he resists the squall of emotion she stirs within him.

Two lonely souls find passion in the turbulent waters of the Atlantic, each a fugitive of their past. As land draws near, Zander is torn between his desire for a woman and his hunger for the sea.

Can love survive once the ship has anchored, or will their newfound happiness founder?

A Medieval Encounter Series

Rolf's Quest

Great Expectations winner, Fire & Ice, Maggie finalist

"Romance, destiny, family values & betrayal all played parts in this intriguing novel that had me turning each page in anticipation."

The BookTweeter

"I enjoyed the flow of the story and the sweet, charming romance. There were unexpected twists and turns that kept my pages turning until the very last page! I highly recommend taking a read through Aubrey's tapestry of Merlin, magic, and true love."

Verified Purchase Review

A wizard, a curse, a fated love...

When Rolf finally discovers the woman who can end the curse that has plagued his family for centuries, she is already betrothed. Time is running out for the royal wizard of King Henry II. If he cannot find true love without the use of sorcery, the magic will die for future generations.

Melissa is intrigued by the mystical, handsome man who haunts her by night and tempts her by day. His bizarre tale of Merlin, enchantments, and finding genuine love has her questioning his sanity and her heart.

From the moment Melissa stepped from his dreams and into his arms, Rolf knew she was his destiny. Now, he will battle against time, a powerful duke, and call on the gods to save her.

Saving Grace (A Small Town Romance)

Contemporary and Colonial America

Holt and Maggie finalist

This unique piece has the reader traveling between the early 1700s and the early 2000s with ease and amazement. The audience truly feels sorrow for Grace and Chloe and is able to connect with each woman for the hardships they are overcoming... The attention to historical facts and details leave one breathless, especially upon learning the people from the past did exist and the memorial erected still stands.

InD'tale Magazine

"I am becoming a pretty decent fan of the author I would say at this point. She managed in such a short amount of pages to thrill me with some lore, romance, and suspense."

Verified Purchase Review

A tortured soul meets a shattered heart...

Chloe Hicks' life consisted of an egocentric ex-husband, a pile of bills, and an equine business in foreclosure until a fire destroys the stable and her beloved ranch horse. What little hope she has left is smashed after the marshal suspects arson. She escapes the accusing eyes of her hometown, but not the memories and melancholy.

Jackson Hahn, Virginia Beach's local historian, has his eyes on the mysterious new woman in town. When she enters his office, he is struck by her haunting beauty and the raw pain in her eyes. Her descriptions of the odd events happening in her bungalow pique his curiosity.

The sexy historian distracts Chloe with the legend of a woman wrongly accused of witchcraft. She is drawn to the story and the similarities of events that plagued their lives. Perhaps the past can help heal the present. But danger lurks in the shadows...

Made in the USA
Monee, IL
13 July 2021

73570533R00111